ideals
GRANDPARENTS

Like the soft, steady glow of the sunlight,
  May your lives continue to shine.
May the years toward tomorrow be richer
  As your interests, devotion, entwine.

        May you, too, shed your light 'long the pathway,
          Guiding others to walk hand in hand.
        May the light of the Father so bless you
          That your joys will be numbered as sand.

    May today be a highlight forever—
      Adding warmth you may constantly share,
    Blessed with loved ones and friends all around you
      And the knowledge God's presence is there.

                            Thelma Anna Martin

Publisher, James A. Kuse
Managing Editor, Ralph Luedtke
Editor/Ideals, Colleen Callahan Gonring
Associate Editor, Linda Robinson
Production Manager, Mark Brunner
Photographic Editor, Gerald Koser
Copy Editor, Norma Barnes
Art Editor, Duane Weaver
Contributing Editor, Beverly Wiersum Charette

ISBN 0-89542-334-0 295

IDEALS—Vol. 37, No. 6 September MCMLXXX. IDEALS (ISSN 0019-137X) is published eight times a year,
January, February, April, June, July, September, October, November
by IDEALS PUBLISHING CORPORATION. 11315 Watertown Plank Road, Milwaukee, Wis. 53226
Second class postage paid at Milwaukee, Wisconsin. Copyright ® MCMLXXX by IDEALS PUBLISHING CORPORATION.
All rights reserved. Title IDEALS registered U.S. Patent Office.
Published Simultaneously in Canada.

ONE YEAR SUBSCRIPTION—eight consecutive issues as published—$15.95
TWO YEAR SUBSCRIPTION—sixteen consecutive issues as published—$27.95
SINGLE ISSUES—$2.95

In Honor
of Grandparents

In 1900 about half of the American households included a mother, father, children and at least one other relative, usually a grandparent. Today, though there are more grandparents on the earth than at any other point in history, most no longer live with their grandchildren.

Conservative estimates are that between twenty-five and thirty percent of our population is made up of grandparents. Almost every child has living grandparents, and many youngsters have all four still alive and able to fill a very rewarding role in the lives of their grandchildren.

The amount of meaningful involvement grandparents have with their grandchildren is often dependent upon how much they feel welcome and needed by the members of their families. It is essential that grandparents enjoy time with their grandchildren, listening to them, showing interest in their many activities, and loving them. The members of these two generations usually have more leisure time than other family members; what better way to spend it than together.

Unfortunately, many older grandparents and great-grandparents are neglected and forgotten. Rabbi Abraham Joshua Haschell has said, "One father finds it possible to sustain a dozen children, yet a dozen children find it impossible to sustain one father." *Sustain*, of course, means more than financial support; it means emotional involvement as well. Parents are responsible for setting an example of loving respect for grandparents, for showing their children that they look up to these older members of their family as beautiful and important people. Caring involvement on all levels is essential to the self-image and mental health of every grandparent.

National Grandparent's Day is of rather recent vintage. While it is true that grandparents also benefit from the observance of Mother's and Father's Day, it seems only fitting and proper that we should set aside a certain day each year in which we honor grandparents for the very special contributions they make to the lives of tomorrow's generation of adults. There are, of course, no long-standing family traditions for Grandparent's Day; there is no legacy of expectations for appropriate behavior. Nevertheless, we can make this Grandparent's Day a day that grandparents of America will remember, and we can continue to give them the joy of our love and attention throughout the year.

Glen Jenson, Ph. D.

"Niagara Falls, next stop, Niagara Falls!"

The conductor's droning monotone released a flood of memories that engulfed me in thoughts of a day long ago: the scent of orange blossoms everywhere, the mellow tones of the organ prelude, the tingling coldness of the ring as it slipped easily onto my finger, the bittersweet taste of the wine and, above all, the radiant face of my new husband. I remembered thinking, "What a wonderful way to start a new life!"

After it was all over, we waited on the train platform, he, pacing, perspiring and glancing at his watch every thirty seconds, I, as cool and fresh as the flowers pinned to my suit coat. When the train pulled in, right on time, we boarded immediately and my husband exhaled a sigh of relief; after making sure that Aunt Emma would eventually get home to Pittsburgh, after thanking everyone twice and kissing them goodbye many times, and after counting our money for at least the thirty-seventh time, we were finally on our way to the honeymoon capital of the world, Niagara Falls.

Niagara Falls
Revisited

We had looked forward to the trip so much that we could not believe it when we found ourselves standing at the brink of one of nature's most breathtakingly powerful forces—Niagara. One of our numerous pamphlets translated the Seneca Indian word "niagara" as "thundering water." It did not take us long to discover just how apt this word was. The first night in our hotel, we thought someone in an adjacent room was taking an unusually long shower until we realized the rumbling noise emanated from the Falls across the river, not a faucet.

For six days we experienced both the American and the Canadian Falls, appreciating from every vantage point their beauty and enduring strength. To prevent getting drenched by the mist constantly rising from the falling water, we donned oversized rain slickers for many of our excursions, and laughingly snapped photos of each other in our "fashionable" apparel. We loved every minute of the trip, and when the time came to head home, we vowed to return some day in the near future.

Well, there we were, forty years later, on our way back to Niagara Falls for an often-planned, and just-as-often-postponed, second honeymoon. The return trip had been delayed by several births, deaths, trips west to Disneyland and the Grand Canyon, weddings and more births.

The train trip from Racine, Wisconsin, to Niagara Falls was smoother, more comfortable, and a great deal shorter than the first one. As we had expected, the area surrounding the cataracts had undergone many changes and additions on both sides of the United States/Canadian border. Our hotel had been replaced by a profusion of modern motels equipped with ice and soda machines, swimming pools and saunas. And yet, in spite of all the commercialism, the overwhelming effect of the Falls remained unchanged. Clinging to the railing, the only barrier separating me from the turbulent water tumbling over the edge of Bridal Veil Falls, I experienced the same feeling of incredulity that overcame me on a similar day so many years past. Like others before, I tried to imagine the sensation of sailing along with the rapid current until abruptly flying over the edge to the foaming depths below, and I shivered at the thought. Yes, Niagara Falls still exerted that hypnotic power I remembered from forty years earlier.

No longer can Niagara Falls be considered the honeymoon capital of the world. With mobility increased by improved transportation, young newlyweds seek more exotic locations to spend their honeymoons. But on the train home I realized that to us, and to the generations of newlyweds who spent their first vacation as husband and wife at this remarkable spot, Niagara Falls will always remain our honeymoon capital.

Rachel Knight

Grandmothers

Grandmothers have magic . . .
How else would they know
The out-of-way places
Where buttercups grow?

The pond in the meadow
Where polliwogs dwell?
The gossip the breezes
Are anxious to tell?

Or how can they tell
By the tracks on the ground
Where hideaway rabbits
And squirrels can be found?

And why do they hug you,
With eyes all aglow,
And tell you the secrets
You're longing to know?

Grandmothers have magic . . .
Or do they recall
The things that were magic
When they were quite small?

Josephine Millard

A Whisker of Pride

All summer
she had waited
for this moment.
Now it was time
to reach into
the unknown.

Growing up is a discarding of dreams—the not-to-be triumphs, the too-dizzying heights, the still-distant horizons. They come in the golden rush of childhood, but they cannot stay. They won't telescope down to the ordinary strictures of time laid out for the chores that need doing.

Yet sometimes, in the long years of burdens, there's a madcap, will-o'-the-wisp moment when—like a child—we can grab at a sparkle in the sky. Reach high for such moments; don't let them pass. For once they are gone they may not come again, and we will have missed a brightness.

All last summer I waited for such a chance, a tiny dream teasing in my mind. Finally it came.

A mile and a half across from our vacation place on Parry Island in Ontario's Georgian Bay lies Palestine Island, a long, dark slope of rock slabs and pine trees. In the evening the sun sets beyond Palestine in a running fire of gold and rose, and then, through a crook in the trees, the distant Carling Rock Lighthouse shines down the night like a blue star.

On a Palestine cliff in a straight line across from our beach is a white house looking small as a cardboard toy, surrounded by shadows. Only rarely does some unseen hand light a lamp so the windows gleam as if a spark of sun had caught in the glass. I had been watching that house over the years; now, suddenly, a desire arose in me—without rhyme or reason, utterly inappropriate—to swim the dark waters to its isolation.

But of course it was ridiculous. I am a grandmother. I have five children. In the world's eye I have done nothing all these years but housework, and we all know that is not conducive to the body beautiful. Although I had come to love swimming, and each summer vacation tried painfully to teach myself the art, it really hadn't worked. Once, when someone told me I was swimming in twenty feet of water, I almost drowned from sudden hysteria.

But that tiny dream kept buzzing through my thoughts. So I began to practice regularly—until "Mother's daily dip" became a family joke. I never missed a day, even in storms, sometimes emerging almost strangled from the banging waves. All the time I was waiting—waiting for strength, for confidence, for a calm day not too cold, and for a scarcity of folks to argue me out of it.

The summer passed without those conditions. Wistfully, I gave up the dream, telling myself I was really too old anyway. Then, late on the last afternoon of vacation, when I was standing on the shore looking out over the water toward the distant, brooding house, the moment came.

The bay was empty of boats since most of the cottagers had already departed. All my family had left, too, save my youngest son. When I dipped my foot in the water, I was surprised it was no colder. The wind of the last two days had died, and the waves were rolling in, easy and gentle. Across the bay the sinking sun was laying a path of gold to my feet, inviting me, urging me, and suddenly, in a lonely calmness, I knew this was my chance to venture into the unknown of what I could do.

I ran back to the cabin where my son was practicing his guitar and rapped on the window.

"I'm swimming to Palestine," I said.

A chord broke off in midair. "Are you crazy?"

"No, serious. Get the canoe, life-jackets, a coat and towel. I've got to hurry. There's only about an hour of daylight left."

I whirled back to the shore and eased into the gold path of sunlight. I swam carefully, testing myself. My muscles felt supple and sure, and I breathed easily.

The sun was skidding into the horizon, dimming my path, when my son, bewildered, paddled up and asked if I was all right.

"Fine," I said, meaning my head included, and swam on, at intervals varying my strokes from breast to back to left and right side.

The darkening distance ahead seemed to stretch implacably, and then the sun went down completely and my path disappeared in the black waters. I had not realized how the cold of the deeper water would eat into my marrow. A layer of numbness ringed my body, and doubts began to arise. Could I finish? Should I keep trying? Was I being foolish?

My son asked me urgently, "Are you cold?"

"No!" A firm lie.

"Are you tired?"

"No!" Another lie.

"Don't you want to turn back?"

"No!" The truth this time.

I swam on, counting strokes, watching for my son's paddle when he pointed it, showing how I was off course. Then I would straighten my line, doggedly trying not to cough or choke, though once a spray of unexpected wake caught me wrong. I no longer looked toward the white house. It stayed too far away, fading into a glimmer shrouded by night.

On and on, and then a little roughness of water and I realized I was in the main channel. I almost laughed. I must be getting there. Overhead the stars were coming out and I watched a scrap of twinkling as though it were a bird leading me on.

Another hundred backstrokes and suddenly I slid into warm, quiet water. I turned over and looked up, and the white house was above my head, a silent, watching presence. Almost languidly I breaststroked into that view, closer and closer. My foot felt the hard cliff shelving under the water and I stood up, and my son was laughing, wrapping my head in his shirt, drying me with a towel, saying over and over, "What a wild, crazy mother you are."

And, oh! I was proud. I had swum to Palestine!

Well, of course, the world with a great whoosh flip-flopped me from the black rock of Palestine back to my winter kitchen and my winter chores of dinner by the clock, proper clothes with functioning zippers and accurate laundering. And that moment of shining pride faded and dwindled until only a whisker remained. And one morning, doing dishes, I wondered if I would forget entirely.

Then, through the window, I saw on my lawn a cobweb from the night—an old lady's cap, we used to call it. And dew hung on it—sparkling drops laced in sunlight-like jewels . . . like jewels dropped from a wind off . . . off Palestine, of course! I smiled in my mind, for I knew then there would be no forgetting. That whisker of pride was mine forever.

Mary Roelofs Stott

My Grandmother's Garden

My grandmother's garden, how well I remember!
  The tall black-eyed susans that grew by the fence,
The ruby-red poppies that glowed like an ember,
  And purple petunias with cinnamon scents.
I can still see the pond and the lilies around it,
  I listen—and bird songs come calling to me.

And there was a pine tree, I know, for I found it,
  Where summer winds whispered, unfettered and free.
The old, stony pathways that ran through the arbor,
  I traveled them all when I played as a child.
In sunshine and shadow I found a safe harbor--
  A retreat for an hour, by cares undefiled.

At night, from my window, I'd throw back the shutter,
  The moon washed with silver, my garden below,
The great summer moths from the shadows would flutter
  And settle on rosebuds as white as the snow.
My grandmother's garden, once ringing with laughter,
  Once filled with the voices of children at play,
I hope that my children, and all who come after
  Will find such a garden—if just for a day!

Hazel Werth

Time spins a magic web of dreams
    Across the crowded years,
I see a host of yesterdays—
    Shadows of smiles and tears.
My heart remembers still the pain,
    Surmounted soon by joy,
In knowing God had shared with me
    A precious baby boy.

I rocked you softly to and fro
    Through lazy summer days,
And pressed you close against my heart
    And soothed your restless ways.
Your eyes were wide and soft and blue,
    Reflecting trust and love,
And as I hummed a lullaby,
    I prayed to God above.

The months went by. You learned to speak;
    And, kneeling by your bed,
I heard in reverent humbleness
    The first prayer that you said.
Your baby steps soon followed me
    Wherever I would go,
And when you fell, I suffered more
    Than you will ever know.

Then came the day we had to bow
    To education's rule;
I caught the tear you didn't see,
    And sent you off—to school.
The years went by. You had your quarrels;
    And mother's heart would yearn
To shield your bruises and your pain,
    But knew you had to learn.

On graduation day, I stood
    Beside your happy Dad
And knew the glow of pride he felt—
    The only son we had.
It wasn't long 'til war came on;
    The country needed men.
My frightened heart stood still, I know,
    Then gave you up again.

Each night I wondered where you camped,
    And prayed most earnestly
That He who gave His only Son
    Would give mine back to me.
And finally the day arrived—
    The war you fought was won!
I clasped you to my breast once more,
    The man who was my son.

You married soon—a lovely girl;
    And yet somehow I knew
A vague and empty loneliness
    At seeing her with you.
But when your little son was born,
    With eyes so soft and blue,
I cradled in my arms again
    The baby that was you.

He snuggled softly at my breast
    As you had often done,
And then I knew it was for this
    That I had shared my son.
And so I rocked him to and fro,
    And prayed a silent prayer
That God should take your little son
    Into His loving care.

And as I pressed him to my heart
    And soothed his restless ways,
I saw across the crowded years
    A host of yesterdays;
My heart remembered still the pain—
    The evil and the good;
But God had given me His best
    In precious motherhood.

A Mother Speaks

Alice Kennelly Roberts

Nostalgic Fragrance

Years ago, Grandmother knew how to save
The lavish gifts summer so freely gave,
Capturing the romance of flowers and sun
(A compensation for work well done).
She gathered rose petals in morning dew,
Rosemary, lavender and violets, too,
Drying them carefully
In friendly shade,
Then, with roots and spices,
She deftly made
A blend of summer,
Captured to bring
A wealth of
Sun-laced remembering
This haunting fragrance
From another day
Was Grandmother's
Rose jar potpourri.

Johanna Ter Wee

In the Beautiful
Garden of Love

I have walked with you
Through the garden of spring
And have lingered there
To hear again
The whispered words
That make the heart sing
In the beautiful garden of love.
You have walked with me
Through the garden of life.
We have lingered there,
Through sunshine and rain,
In the season where blossoms
Of love grew rife
In the beautiful garden
Of love.
So we walk with joy
Through the garden today
And we linger, alone,
To hear again
The songs from the heart,
Along the pathway
In the beautiful garden
Of love.

Lucy Munro Barker

I Would Go with You

Because you walk through ways of charm and beauty,
I would go with you down the lanes of time;
My glad heart leaps as to a call of duty,
As poet pens, it speaks the beat of rhyme.
Because you lead matched minds to epic meeting
In gardens that are given to fair thought,
Bright joy, like rainbows, is mine for the keeping,
Alive are dreams that my soul deeply sought.
Because you picture life as good and treasured,
Mankind, a valued occupant of earth,
Closer seem the merits time has measured,
Clearer are the images of worth.
Sweet inspiration thrives while beauty reigns;
I would go with you down ethereal lanes.

Maxine McCray Miller

Grandparents

Ottis Shirk

It's funny how grandparents sometimes act
    When their first grandchild arrives,
But often little things will make
    Great changes in our lives.

While talking one day, it was Grandma said,
    "I know I'll never bar
Those darling, little, chubby hands
    From Grandma's cookie jar."

Then Grandpa, with a heart of love,
    Spoke these words in between,
"I'll never once refuse to buy
    Him candy or ice cream."

Grandma continued, "I'll sure be glad
    When he begins to crawl,
And leaves his little fingerprints
    On furniture and wall."

"And Grandpa won't refuse to spend,
    If it will bring him joy,
The last cent in his pocket,
    For some simple, little toy."

Thus they talked for quite a while,
    When Mother came along
And said, "If you did all those things,
    I think it would be wrong."

Grandparents must remember
    If it's true love they would show,
For baby's good, there's many times
    They'll have to answer, "No."

The arrival of a new baby is surely one of life's most marvelous events. If fills us with awe and wonder, and when we participate in it as grandparents it adds an exhilarating new dimension to our lives.

We hold it in our arms, tantalized by the ineffable mystery of its inheritance, to which we, too, have added our bit. This is no little empty vessel, as we used to be told, no little hollow pitcher into which we will pour the ingredients of a new personality. We know now that it comes to us with its mind already made up, as one might say, its unique genetic endowment already encoded for the kind of person it is capable of becoming.

Looking into the tiny, wizened face of the newborn—so transiently prophetic of the future adult—we search for family resemblances, try to guess at family traits and talents hidden there. Whom will this enigmatic little person take after? What novel blend of our pooled characteristics will it reveal?

In all the excitement of its arrival, the hustle and bustle of welcoming it into the world, we can scarcely stop to think what its coming can actually mean to us, its grandparents. Only later, when we have helped to see to its comfort, do we begin to realize what has happened to us. Our first grandchild is the herald of a new phase in our lives, and every grandchild that comes after will reaffirm the wonder of it.

Our grandchildren expand and enhance our lives in ways that reach deep. They reach back into our past and far into our future. They re-create old joys for us, and promise ever new ones as they grow. As for our present, they can enrich the hours and days if we wish, and as much as we wish. As grandparents we have the choice, always, of how much or how little we are involved with them, and even a little involvement—the one or two visits a year if they live far away—can bring very special pleasures.

Each one of our grandchildren is a fresh, unique experience, a new personality, a small but definite individual with whom we can forge a bond. If we are shy with babies, soon enough we find them toddlers, conversationalists on the telephone, crayon artists sending us pictures, school children writing us awkwardly formed words in block letters and original spellings, teenagers confiding to us their adolescent joys and griefs. We can enter their lives at any stage with which we feel comfortable. And we enter with an ideal introduction, a passport second only to that of their parents. We are their grandparents.

What we can do for them we learn as we go along—from them, from their parents, from our own feelings and insights, from other grandparents. Grandparents are forever exchanging pictures and stories with other grandparents, and we garner wisdom from others' experience.

What they do for us also comes as a discovery. Grandmothers of long standing speak of it as a second chance. They remember the dreadful mistakes they made, or think they made, as parents, and their grandchildren give them the opportunity to re-create themselves in a more satisfying parental image. This time they are able to say and do the right things, as perhaps they did not, the first time around. And not because they are older, more experienced in life, possibly wiser, but because they are that one delicious step removed from the hourly and daily pressures and responsibilities of child-rearing.

But there is much more that our grandchildren do for us. They rekindle for us the spirit of play, the child's sense of adventure and discovery. Grandparents are always being told that they are living history to their grandchildren, that they give the children the reassurance of their roots, the strengthening awareness of continuity. For me and many grandmothers I have talked to, it works the other way as well. Grandchildren give us continuity. They link us to our own motherhood and childhood years, to our parents and grandparents and the stories we remember of times even earlier than those. And they link us to the future as well. They give us a vested interest in the world in which they will live. They make us aware of the world in which we are living today and helping to create for tomorrow.

And all this at our own choice. We choose how far and how deep our grandparenthood will take us. For perhaps the first time in our lives, as grandparents we have the freedom to take as little or as much as we desire out of this new facet of living that our grandchildren bring to us.

Reprinted with permission of Macmillan Publishing Co., Inc. from A Book for Grandmothers by Ruth Goode. Copyright © 1976 by Ruth Goode.

Ruth Goode

Just Like Grandparents

There's something very warm about a grandparent-child relationship. Grandmas are notorious for their innate ability to spoil their grandchildren—"Oh, let him have another. I just baked them this morning"—and grandpas have the safest laps in the world when it's storytelling time.

Our three sons never knew their grandparents. Unfortunately, neither my parents nor my husband's lived long enough to share in our children's lives. I remember when each of the boys would come home from kindergarten, young and vulnerable, asking why everyone else had a grandma and grandpa "except me." It was difficult to answer the sad question: "Katie's always going to her grandma's for Easter. How come we can't go to *our* grandma's?"

Although our sons never had "real" grandparents, we have been singularly blessed in knowing many older people who, through the years, became delightful surrogate grandparents. Lily, the mother of a friend of ours, likes nothing better than to sit down and deal several hands of cards with the boys. She's a sassy, peppery 83-year-old with a hearty laugh and a splendid sense of humor. She's tickled pink when she trumps somebody's ace, and she cracks a lot of jokes in her rich, southern-Indiana accent. She never ceases to amaze us, and we all love her as much as we could love a natural grandmother.

When the boys were very young, we rented a large, older, lower flat. The landlady, Mrs. Peabody, lived upstairs with her grown son. Although she was nearly crippled with arthritis, her spirit was unconquerable. She had to use a walker to get around her kitchen, but that didn't stop her from baking each year, with the help of her granddaughters, literally thousands of Christmas cookies.

Without fail, every Christmas Eve we would receive a beautiful red tin of "Grandma Peabody's" delicious, fancy delicacies. Every Christmas morning we feasted on one of her homemade holiday stollens. "I make a dozen every year and give them all away," she'd say with a smile. The years have passed, and Mrs. Peabody is gone; but there's never a Christmas morning when we don't remember her.

Easter was another of her favorite holidays, and she would bake for days before her family gathered for dinner. It was traditional for her to call us the day before Easter with a whispered request that we bring up the boys' Easter baskets "so the Bunny can put in a little surprise." Sure enough, every Easter their baskets would hold homemade chocolate-coconut nests with tiny jelly bird eggs inside — a special treat they've never forgotten.

One of our dearest "substitute" grandmothers is a feisty Irish lady in her late seventies. A registered nurse, Susan earned the rank of colonel in the air force during World War II. For years our boys were fascinated with her endless stories, told in a sparkling Irish brogue. Now, she never fails to have a positive comment about our sons: "Ah, sure he's a fine lad, and you'll not have to worry about him." There are times when I wish I shared her loving confidence.

Elderly neighbors have been a constant delight. One stormy Lithuanian grandma used to work diligently in her garden, keeping an eye on the neighborhood while she attacked the weeds. If she saw our oldest boy, then about four, tease his two-year-old brother, she'd shout, "You! Be nice to brother!" Then, afraid she had been too harsh, she'd present each child with a homemade cookie — and the biggest grin they'd ever seen.

As parents of young children, we were often concerned that the boys would annoy some of our older neighbors with their mischief. We needn't have worried. There always seemed to be an unspoken bond of friendship between the generations; if one of our sons ran to the store for an older neighbor, he was invariably rewarded with a Popsicle and a hug. Our youngest son came home proudly one hot summer day holding a shiny new dime. He happily announced that he had "a job" — helping Mr. and Mrs. Hady sprinkle their lawn! I'm sure they didn't really need a helper, but it was a kind and generous gesture on their part.

Pete, a young 75-year-old who lived down the block, was a master of the art of teasing. It wasn't unusual to catch him, during a July block party, hiding behind a tree and gleefully shooting all the neighborhood children with a squirt gun. He had just as much fun on the receiving end, too, darting away and laughing when the youngsters returned his "fire." He made regular visits to the rabbit cage in our backyard and always brought a bunch of dandelions as a treat for Duncan — whom he insisted on calling "Charlie."

Our boys have learned some valuable lessons through their acquaintances with these remarkable older people. They know that sorrow is part of every life, but so is laughter; they've learned that imperfections can be tolerated and that blessings must be counted. They've learned about a generosity of spirit that they realize is far more important than mere generosity with material things.

When we reminisce with family photo albums, the boys still ask questions about their grandparents. I wish they could have known my parents and my husband's parents. But since that was not meant to be, we're grateful that, in this case at least, a substitute is almost as good as the real thing.

Bea Bourgeois

Unfoldment

Let us think of each day as a flower
Unfolding in sunshine's warm light,
An opening bud in the morning,
A beautiful blossom at night.

The hours, like fairest-hued petals
Unfolding in God's tender love,
Reflecting His beauty and goodness
In thoughts that come from above.

And, flowerlike, breathing out fragrance
To all who may come our glad way,
The Father's compassion and sweetness
Touching all that we do or say.

And when night's golden stars look downward,
And soft, cooling dew fills the air,
May we see our day as a flower . . .
God's own, and divinely fair.

Ella A. Stone

Autumn

When Autumn comes in all her regal finery
And coloring, which sets the world aflame,
Her spicy breath whispers of nature's winery,
Her voice is filled with sounds of calling game.

When Autumn comes, her happy footsteps rustle;
Her companion is Jack Frost, upon her arm.
And he etches gleaming crystal, as they bustle
Through visits to each city, town and farm.

When Autumn comes and brilliant leaves go flying
And fill the air across the golden fields,
It is not long until the cold wind's sighing
Heralds the scythe which lonely Winter wields.

But Autumn comes! Each year her beauty splashes
The countryside with lovely, flaming wings.
And God, through her resplendent flashes,
Reveals His love, and all the joy it brings.

Marian Benedict Manwell

Glenn Ward Dresbach

Glenn Ward Dresbach has been called "The Poet of the West and Southwest." Many of his poems reflect the rugged atmosphere of that part of the country. Born in 1889 on a farm in Lanark, Illinois, Dresbach gained recognition early in his writing career as a student at the University of Wisconsin. As a young man, Dresbach was determined to become a poet. He combined his writing talents with a career in business, working as an accountant during the day and on his poetry at night. Dresbach strove to develop a technique that would suit his subject matter, believing that a poet should be able to communicate intelligently to a wide audience. As the young poet gained recognition, his poems appeared in the best literary and popular magazines as well as major newspapers. Today, his work is included in almost two hundred anthologies and textbooks. Dresbach also received over one hundred literary awards in his lifetime, including the Poetry Society of Texas Award in 1928 for one of his best collections, *Star Dust and Stone.* The American author believed that the poet should be a "complete person in contact with the world" and everything relating to human experience. Before his death in 1968 at his Ozark mountain home in Eureka Springs, Arkansas, Dresbach was acclaimed as a poet who transcended regional and national boundaries and spoke for all people.

Wild Geese Over the Desert

From sunset, slowly fading
To misted beryl and blue
Streaked with the melted topaz,
The goose-wedge comes in view.

The boughs of twisted cedars
On ledges darkly sway,
Making a futile gesture
To rise and fly away.

Nothing will have beginning
And nothing end in me,
For watching the geese fly over,
That anyone may see.

Only my heart makes gesture
Of lifting wings to go,
Like boughs of the twisted cedars
Dark on a fading glow.

Giving

Life has two ways of giving: from the one
We keep a little while the golden light,
Love's nearness, and a shelter from the night,
Our fields to sow and reap, with rain and sun.
We fill our bins and mows but that is done
In vain if hearts be empty, if the flight
Of wings made skies no clearer to our sight,
If we but pause where vision had begun.

Life has two ways of giving: from the other
We keep the only permanence we know
By sharing treasures that we hold in trust . . .
Song for the songless, raiment for another,
And food, where torrents and the tempests go,
And dreams to star again the mortal dust!

The Last Corn Shock

I remember how we stood
In the field, while far away
Blue hazes drifted on from hill to hill
And curled like smoke from many a sunset wood,
And the loaded wagon creaked while standing still . . .
I heard my father say,
"The last corn shock can stay."

We had seen a pheasant there
In the sun; he went inside
As if he claimed the shock, as if he meant
To show us, with the field so nearly bare,
We had no right to take his rustic tent.
And so we circled wide
For home, and let him hide.

The first wild ducks flashed by
Where the pasture brook could hold
The sunset at the curve, and drifting floss
Escaped the wind and clung. The shocks were dry
And rustled on the wagon. Far across
The field, against the cold,
The last shock turned to gold.

Autumn Crickets

A drowsy music drifts across the dusk
Where crickets fiddle fore wings out of tune
With half-heard threnodies of grass and husk
And leaf-waves breaking on the low, red moon.
This is the music that we heard below
The opened rose, in harmony with all
The fragrant rhythms of the night, the slow
Dance of the moonlight on a flowered wall.

Beneath the shadow-dances of the grass
Earth-pulses throbbed in these articulate wings.
They stay . . . though on this night the witch-clouds pass
Above the pathways of departing things.
We find, where shadow circles now are drawn,
The music playing . . . and the dancers gone.

Autumn Garden

She tucks her flowers in their beds—
Like other little sleepyheads
So long ago! Her tired, old fingers
Touch them so gently, and she lingers
By each bed. And the frost tonight
Will stitch these coverlets in white
Chilled patterns—but the roses sleep
In leafy blankets, pansies keep
Bright faces pressed to quilts of moss,
And pinks will feel no chill across
Their covering of brown and gold
She made of leaves. Though she is old
She thinks of other sleepyheads . . .
So long ago . . . while in their beds
She tucks her flowers, late today,
Smiles to herself and turns away—
With memories like a garden in
Her heart, where faithful love has been
The gardener. And there she talks
With One who in that garden walks.

September Watercolor

The willows drop the yellow leaves
They can no longer hold—
Irreverent, the blackbirds strut
Upon a cloth of gold.

Below them silver of a brook
Runs through a meadow strange
Too suddenly, and fades in blue
Hazed atmosphere of change. . . .

The airs are still, but here I feel
A movement in my heart,
Like phantom hands reached out to stay
Beauty that must depart.

In the early 1900s Milton Snavely Hershey began mass-producing chocolate, putting his cocoa products in the cupboards of almost every household in America. By the early 1930s, Hershey's Baking Chocolate was probably a very familiar and necessary ingredient in many rich devil's food cakes or creamy chocolate pies.

Remember when your neighbor called to share with you her favorite recipe for chocolate cake? That great old-time recipe and many others for delicious chocolate desserts can probably still be found tucked away on the shelves in your kitchen. Why not rediscover them and delight your family with an old-fashioned treat on their next visit? You can be sure there will be plenty of eager volunteers to lick the bowls clean when you bake with chocolate. Your grandchildren may ask you to share the recipes for your favorite chocolate desserts. It's likely they already know the secret to that luscious homemade flavor is the ingredient you never fail to add—love!

CHOCOLATE CARAMEL SAUCE

1 cupful brown sugar, packed . . . dash of salt . . . 3 tablespoonfuls water . . . ¼ cupful Hershey's Chocolate Flavored Syrup . . . 1 tablespoonful butter . . . 1 tablespoonful cornstarch . . . 1 cupful hot water . . . ½ teaspoonful vanilla.

Cook the sugar and salt with 3 tablespoonfuls water to a light caramel brown. Remove from heat; add chocolate syrup, then the butter and cornstarch, mixed to a paste, and the hot water. Cook over direct heat until thick (220°F.), about 15 minutes; add vanilla. Serve with cottage pudding or any hot dessert. This sauce is very nice with ice cream.

Yield: 1 cupful sauce.

COCOA PEPPERMINT ICING

½ cupful butter . . . ½ cupful Hershey's Cocoa . . . 3⅔ cupfuls (1-pound box) 4X sugar (confectioners') . . . 7 tablespoonfuls milk . . . 1 teaspoonful vanilla . . . 1 tablespoonful crushed peppermint candy.

Melt the butter in a saucepan; add the cocoa and heat 1 minute or until smooth, stirring constantly. Alternately add sugar and milk, beating to spreading consistency. Blend in vanilla and peppermint candy.

Yield: About 2¼ cupfuls icing or enough for an 8- or 9-inch layer cake.

Hershey poster from the 1930s

DEVILS' DELIGHT CAKE

4 squares Hershey's Baking Chocolate, melted . . . ⅔ cupful brown sugar, packed . . . 1 cupful milk . . . 1 egg yolk . . . ⅓ cupful butter . . . ½ cupful brown sugar, packed . . . 2 egg yolks . . . 2 cupfuls sifted cake flour . . . ¼ teaspoonful salt . . . 1 teaspoonful baking soda . . . ½ cupful milk . . . 1 teaspoonful vanilla . . . 3 egg whites . . . ½ cupful brown sugar, packed.

Combine melted baking chocolate with ⅔ cupful brown sugar, 1 cupful milk and 1 beaten egg yolk, and stir over simmering water until well blended. Cool slightly. Cream butter, then add ½ cupful brown sugar gradually, while beating constantly. Add 2 egg yolks, well-beaten. Sift flour, salt and baking soda 3 times, and add to creamed mixture alternately with ½ cupful milk, beating thoroughly. Add chocolate mixture and vanilla, and beat. Beat egg whites until foamy; gradually add ½ cupful brown sugar and beat until stiff. Fold into batter. Pour into 2 buttered and floured 9-inch round cake pans. Bake in a moderate oven (350 degrees) for 35 minutes. Spread layers and top with any favorite frosting, and cover with thinly sliced oranges sprinkled with minced nutmeats and minced citron or candied ginger.

A Kiss for You

HERSHEY'S KISSES

HERSHEY, PA A Town

Built on Chocolate

There is hardly a person in this country who doesn't associate the name *Hershey* with chocolate. But how many people know about the quaint little town in central Pennsylvania that bears the same name? Hershey, PA , affectionately called, "The Chocolate Town," has the distinctive quality of being one of the most beautiful and charming "factory towns" in the U.S.

It's not hard to guess what "sweet" product is produced in the factory which dominates the locale's industry. This, of course, is the home of the famous Hershey's Milk Chocolate Bars, candies and other goodies which most Americans have enjoyed since the turn of the century.

The man who gave his name to the chocolate bars and the town was Milton Snavely Hershey, the only child of industrious, plain-living Pennsylvania farmers of Swiss origin. As a young man, Milton made attempts to establish himself as a confectioner in Philadelphia, Chicago, Denver and New York before returning to Lancaster County, Pennsylvania, where he grew up, and opening a candy business, specializing in caramels. His caramels were well received by the public, and his business finally prospered. In 1900, he sold his caramel company, and at the age of forty-two, became an instant millionaire. Although well-heeled for life, he felt compelled by a growing interest in the manufacture of chocolate to strike out into a new business venture.

In 1893, Mr. Hershey visited the World's Fair in Chicago and became interested in the German chocolate-making machinery on display there. He purchased the machinery and took it home, spending many hours tinkering with it and experimenting with the difficult task of making real milk chocolate. After much trial and error, Hershey worked out his own formula for making chocolate.

Now, he needed to build a factory to accommodate the new chocolate industry which he was sure would grow. He believed that the wisest approach to making his chocolate would be to mass produce a single product—the Hershey's Milk Chocolate Bar—and make it accessible to everyone by selling it at a low price. Before that time, chocolate was made in limited quantities and was an expensive commodity.

In 1903, Mr. Hershey began building his chocolate factory in the cornfields of Lebanon Valley, a lush and picturesque stretch of land nestled between the low and hazy Blue Mountains. People scoffed at the idea of building a factory miles from any urban area, but Milton Hershey probably envisioned, even then, the bright and happy community that would grow side by side with his chocolate factory in the idyllic surroundings of Derry Township.

As the chocolate factory began to rise, Mr. Hershey immediately saw the need for a railroad station and made sure that one was promptly built. Soon after, he constructed a post office and trolley system. In laying out the town, Mr. Hershey did not follow the general plan of the average nineteenth century industrial town. He wanted each home to have its own surrounding lawn or garden and encouraged an attractive mixture of architecture on every block. Instead of the usual Main Street, he named the two major thoroughfares, Chocolate Avenue and Cocoa Avenue. Other streets were

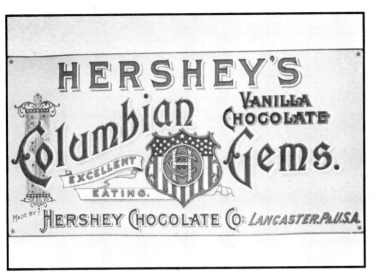

Reproduction of an early Hershey product label

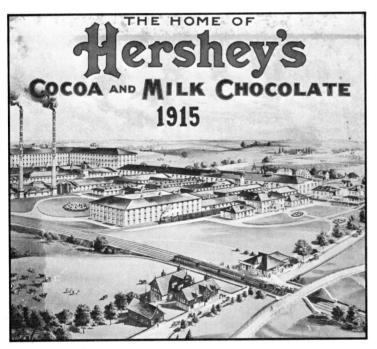

Hershey promotion circa 1915

given the distinctive names of Caracas, Granada, Areba, Trinidad, Para, Java and Ceylon—cities and countries from which cocoa beans are imported.

As the town grew in population, Mr. Hershey kept on building. He had a meeting house constructed for employees of his factory, a fire station, and in later years, a bank, department store, hotel, recreational center, utilities and schools. He also laid out an amusement park, golf course, zoo, outdoor theater and dancing pavilion, all beautifully designed and surpassing those found in many larger cities.

Milton Hershey had once made the statement that he did not return to business to increase his worldly possessions, but for the satisfaction of doing something worthwhile and for the benefit of others. As further proof of this pledge, he opened a school for orphaned boys, which today has grown into one of the finest such facilities in the entire country.

A sports arena was added to the community in the thirties, and in 1937, the employees of the chocolate company gave a huge party in the new arena to celebrate Milton Hershey's eightieth birthday. At that time, he was still living in his home—Highpoint Mansion—after giving the building to the local country club and retaining a small apartment for himself. Today, the mansion serves as the headquarters of the Hershey Foods Corporation.

Even in his later years, M.S., as the community affectionately called him, continued overseeing production at the chocolate factory and experimenting with new ways of extracting more beneficial products from the wondrous cocoa bean. He lived to celebrate his eighty-eighth birthday, but died shortly after on October 13, 1945.

Today, the town of Hershey is a microcosm of culture in the middle of the state of Pennsylvania, bringing music, theater, dance and education to many people. Its beautiful amusement center—Hersheypark—draws thousands of tourists from around the country each year. Mr. Hershey incorporated this park into his original plans for the town, and it gave much pleasure and relaxation to the early citizens of the community. In 1971, the park underwent total redevelopment. It retains the original gracious spirit and natural beauty but with an added flavor of the cultural heritage indigenous to central Pennsylvania. Visitors can see Pennsylvania Dutch craftsmen demonstrating their skills and displaying their creations. There are also rides, restaurants, exhibits, shows and a zoo featuring plant and animal life from around the world.

When Milton Hershey built his chocolate factory in a cornfield, some people called him unwise and a dreamer. But he was a man with a vision that extended far beyond conventional horizons—a vision that saw the realization of one of the loveliest, most imaginative and livable towns in the United States.

Michele Arrieh

A Remarkable Period

Ellen Naughton

I am nearing my eightieth birthday, and my mind is crowded with memories as it takes me back to my childhood years in the early 1900s. Growing up was a truly wonderful experience for me. I could not have been happier.

I was born of Irish descent in Liverpool, England, in 1899. Liverpool was called little Ireland. It was a thriving seaport with factories, mills and other manufacturing establishments on the periphery of the city. My family and our friends all lived there. We were working-class people.

I followed with interest the evolution of the new inventions that were being developed. The mechanical age had arrived, and I spent many pleasant and curious hours sitting on the curbstone with my peers watching the mechanics from the motor-works testing the new motor cars on the main street. It was fascinating. On these occasions the horses and teams used the side streets.

Edison's cylindrical recording machines, which had been in great favor, were losing out to Victor recording machines. Victor was using flat discs, and some of the greatest artists from the opera world, as well as the best performers in legitimate theater, were recording for them. Someone donated a Victor machine to the school I attended, and each Friday afternoon at the end of the school day, everyone gathered in the assembly hall to listen to the records. The teachers were as interested as the children. I looked forward to this time with great joy.

Electricity was a power to be reckoned with. I remember very clearly sitting astride my father's shoulders, watching in amazement as the first electrically illuminated car made a trial run through the city. It was early in the evening, and both sides of the streets were lined with people. After the car had passed by, everyone was strangely silent. I could not understand it at the time, but since I have grown older, I have come to think that the adults must have sensed a great change in the future. The children, naturally, took it in stride. Any change was fun for them.

The introduction of American moving pictures was an innovation that brought a great deal of pleasure into most people's lives, especially the children's. The Saturday afternoon matinee became a way of life for many of them. Rain or shine, the playground was deserted in favor of the matinee.

These motion pictures left strong impressions. The U.S.A. symbolized hope for the working class, as people had a chance to see how some Americans lived. The ranches in the west were a revelation to them. Every Saturday afternoon the children rode the American plains in fantasy with the cowboys. I know they loved to watch the huge herds of cattle and the beautiful horses. While my companions and I derived great pleasure from watching the race horses train in the paddock, it was never so satisfying as watching the panorama of the west on Saturday afternoon at the moving picture show.

Man's inventions were not all that made life exciting in those days. Time moved on. It was the first of May, 1910. Everyone was excited about the return of Halley's comet, which was expected on the twenty-fourth. Like everyone else, I was looking forward to this phenomenon expectantly.

At the time, I was ten years old and very curious, as were most of my friends, about the sky and the comet's origin. We all wanted to know more about it and were very happy one day to see a notice on the school bulletin board advising all students to gather in the assembly hall at a designated time for a brief explanation of the comet's behavior. It was then that we learned of Halley's part in the discovery of the comet.

According to historians, Edmund Halley was born in England in 1656. In 1682, like other scientists in other parts of the world, he was very much interested in a lone comet that was traveling outside the solar system and very close to the earth. While all other celestial bodies traveled around the sun in the same direction, this comet was unique. It went the opposite way.

Halley was very much interested and traced the comet's source. After much research, he discovered that it was the same comet which had been seen close to earth in 1456, 1531 and 1607. He recorded his sighting of the comet and, in due time, he heard from other scientists.

Since travel was not easy in those days, it was a long time before the scientists could meet and compare their findings. While there was agreement that they all might have seen the same comet, they did not continue to pursue its course. Halley did, though, and found that he had been correct in his deductions. He also believed that the comet of 1682 was possibly the same one that had been seen in 450 B.C. and that it might well return again in about 76 years.

Continuing to research diligently, he predicted the comet's return in 1758. Although Halley died in 1742 and did not see proof of the accuracy of his prediction, others did, and an international group of scientists, who knew how hard he had worked to trace the comet's origin, decided to honor Halley posthumously by naming the comet for him.

On the morning of the expected arrival of the comet, the sun shone with an unusual brilliance. When I met my companions on the way to school, the first thing they mentioned was the brightness of the sun.

As we all neared the school building, a pale yellow haze spread over the sky. The school bell was ringing, signaling the children to cease play, join the lines that were forming, and go into the classrooms. My friends and I joined the proper lines and moved with everyone else into the building. All the children stayed inside just long enough to be registered, after which we returned to the school-yard to wait excitedly for the comet.

There was a tall, iron-railed fence around the school building, and I remember how surprised and glad I was to see one of the local glaziers on the sidewalk, distributing blackened pieces of glass through the open railings, so that everyone could see the comet more clearly.

He had placed his handcart on the side of the road near the curbstone. It was filled with glass and equipped with a glass cutter and torch. Anyone of us who did not have a piece of glass was making herself heard. When he was satisfied that everyone was supplied, he sat on the side of his handcart and waited with the rest of us for the comet.

Everyone watched in quiet suspense as the sky became increasingly dark, until one could sense the approaching comet. In a matter of seconds, it came flashing into view, looking like a large fish, bright green and orange in color, becoming a misty gray at the tail.

The tail was very wide and trailed for yards in a long, wavering motion, until it scattered into oblivion, and the sky resumed its natural color. It was all over in minutes.

Although I knew that it would pass quickly, I was disappointed when it did not linger. Still, while it lasted, it was a wonderful sight. I do not remember the exact time of the comet's passing, but all the children and teachers were back in the classroom before eleven o'clock. It had begun to rain, which everyone expected, and it continued all day. No

doubt, the comet disturbed the elements. As I recall our class did not do any serious school work for the rest of the morning.

Halley's comet made such an impression on me, that I think I shall remember it for the rest of my life. It is due again in 1986. I hope I shall live long enough to see it.

It is true that there have been a considerable number of changes in this old world since Halley's comet returned in 1910. Two world wars and numerous conflicts between nations have brought suffering to millions. The many inventions that were developed, however, have also brought comfort to the sick and ease to many.

We can thank the inventors, before and after the turn of the century, for the self-discipline they must have imposed on themselves, to build the first airplane, automobile, radio and television. They laid the groundwork for those who came after them, for those who have improved upon and developed any number of wonderful things.

We cannot all invent great things, and the events of our lives are not always historic. Nevertheless, since I have reached my present age I have discovered that with good health, the greatest gift one can receive from the Creator, one can accomplish much. Life is a challenge, and all any mortal can do is "have a go at it."

Celebrate

Thanksgiving
with *ideals* . . .

- Trace our forefathers' journey to America's shores.

- Enjoy color photography that captures our nation's beauty in brilliant autumn foliage.

- Learn all about the cranberry—savor prize-winning recipes featuring this tangy native fruit.

- **Celebrate Thanksgiving with Ideals—subscribe today for yourself or as a gift to a special friend.**

Bless My Home

Carice Williams

Fill my home, dear Lord, I pray,
  With blessings from above,
But . . . most of all . . . I ask that it
  Be always filled with love.

May those who step within my door
  Find happy hearts inside.
And, Lord, please may my door and heart
  Be ever open wide.

May all who gather round my hearth
  Find kindness glowing there,
And may each soul who dwells within,
  Love and contentment share.

So, bless my home and bless each one
  Who dwells or steps inside,
And may I find beneath my roof
  That peace and joy abide.

When I'm a Grandma, Too

I hope when I'm a grandma, too,
  My hands will find small jobs to do,
Like knitting sweaters, making toys,
  And gingerbread men for little boys,
A doll to dress for a small girl
  And flaxen hair to softly curl.

I hope I have a doughnut crock
  And red striped peppermints in stock,
White aprons trimmed with homemade lace,
  A kitten by the fireplace,
A hob to set a kettle on,
  With rosy curtains snugly drawn.

I hope that I shall have a yard,
  Where crimson hollyhocks stand guard
Near a small bed of mignonette.
  That I shall have small meals to get,
Using my Sunday chinaware
  With roses on the bill of fare.

That children, as they come along,
  Will sense somehow that they belong
To all the beauty gathered here,
  And feel themselves beloved and dear,
Beyond all language to convey,
  Sheltered and guarded at their play.

I hope that I shall prove to be
  All that they ever hoped of me.

Edna Jaques

The Portrayal

Loise Pinkerton Fritz

Upon a tree stump, dark with age,
An old man sat, while brightest rays
Of sunshine filtered through the trees,
And on his furrowed brow the breeze
Touched gently every line etched there
By years of toil for family dear.

Upon his knee a boy of three
Snuggled close and endlessly
Asked these questions: "Why the trees?"
"Why the sunshine?" . . . "Why the breeze?"
While patiently the old man tried
To take each question in his stride
And answer each as best he could
According to the Holy Book.

An arm's length from the stump that day
I saw so lovingly portrayed
The age-old generation gap . . .
A little child on Grandpa's lap.

Grandfather, dear, what a long, long time
Since you were small like me,
I wonder how you remember still
What the life of a child must be;
Yet, when I look in your kind, old eyes,
And feel of your wrinkled hand,
The cling is there like the cling of mine,
And I know you can understand.
I know it's only the four-score years
That have put the snow in your hair,
And that, just like mine, in the heart of yours,
Is the love-light burning there.
I want my life to be full like yours,
That when I am old like you,
I may know the joy of the wintertime,
And live in my children, too.

Bertha A. Kleinman

Grandfather

Grandma's House

Grandma's house is special,
And when we go to visit
We never have to phone ahead;
She doesn't ask, "Who is it?"

She somehow seems to know it's us,
And that we love to come,
For visiting at Grandma's house
Is lots more fun than home.

It isn't just the cookies,
Or the different toys we get—
It's not just fun with Grandpa,
Or the dog and cat to pet;

It's not just snuggling quietly,
And rocking in her chair—
But Grandma's house is special
Because my grandma's there.

Marian Benedict Manwell

On Becoming a Grandmother

So now I'm a grandmother, God, and I am truly grateful.

Awe fills me. A sense of excited achievement. I want to laugh, I want to sing, I want to go down on my knees.

I also want to cry. For sheer delight, yes, and for tenderness. But also just a little bit for me.

A part of me isn't quite ready to be a grandmother, God. A vain, silly, private-life-hugging part of me.

The very word sounds so final. Old. Smacking of rocking chairs and easy slippers. Of being shooed into a corner to bake the cookies, knit the mittens or merely dandle grandchildren on my lap.

And that isn't true anymore. Not for most women—and, oh, God, don't let it be for me.

However I adore this grandchild and will love those to come, don't let me become too absorbed in it. Let me keep my own work, my own interests, my own identity.

(Come to think of it, everybody will be better off if I just keep on being me.)

And now that I've confessed my reservations, let me accept this new phase of my life proudly.

Grandmother . . . I will grasp and savor the true beauty of that word—its grandeur and its glory. To be a grand—mother. What a compliment. May I live up to it.

Thank you, God, for revealing the wonder of becoming a grandmother to me.

Marjorie Holmes

Legacy!

He walked along
A magic path
With her, whose father
Was his son,
And mused upon
The many years
Since it had
All begun:

The legend
Of the talking wood,
The fairy
Kingdom glen . . .
Her elfin eyes
Danced sheer delight
And raced across
A thousand nights
When she would
Dream again.
The path of promise,
Paved with joy,
Her granddad found
While still a boy.
She need not know
'Twas fashioned lore
To please a little
Child of four!

Merry Browne

Daisies for My Lady

My bride, my bride, of fifty-nine years,
Sharing laughter, sharing tears,
Growing together, becoming as one,
The fruits of our love, our daughter, our son.
Long days of toil, brief times of rest,
Working together, our lives have been blessed,
Now, even grandchildren have babes of their own,
Can it be? Our grandchildren are really full-grown?
And yet my sweet lady, your beauty remains,
Your voice still is lilted with girlish refrains.
While others are troubled with differences many,
We can thank our dear Lord, we scarce have had any.
So I bring you wild daisies, in the hope they will tell,
How you've brightened each day by your love lived so well.

Margaret Macdonald

We Have Lived
and Loved Together

We have lived and loved together
Through many changing years;
We have shared each other's gladness
And wept each other's tears;
I have known ne'er a sorrow
That was long unsoothed by thee;
For thy smiles can make a summer
Where darkness else would be.

Like the leaves that fall around us
In autumn's fading hours,
Are the traitor's smiles, that darken
When the cloud of sorrow lowers;
And, though many such we've known, love,
Too prone, alas, to range,
We both can speak of one love
Which time can never change.

We have lived and loved together
Through many changing years,
We have shared each other's gladness
And wept each other's tears.
And let us hope the future,
As the past has been will be:
I will share with thee my sorrows,
And thou, thy joys with me.

Charles Jefferys

Time is a measure
Of hearts that give,
Of lives that live . . .
Time is a treasure.

Time is a key
That opens the mind
Of all mankind
To deep eternity.

Time is a pod
That holds the seed
Of every need
Created by God.

Margie Lee Johnson

Time's Souvenir

June Masters Bacher

A golden treasure's buried here
Mid souvenirs of mine—
Grandpa's faithful, old pocket watch,
His measurement of time.
Symbolically, the shining chain
From engraved case to fob,
Unbroken, like his loyalty,
Half-century on the job.
The timepiece a grand token was
For all the years he'd spent
In the small town's only bank—
The cash and kindness lent.
He used to wrap the chain around
His fingers as he talked
And check the front-vest-pocket time
As down the street he walked.
At five A.M. he would arise,
Take down his moustache cup
And, pouring rich brown coffee, say,
"I'll wake the roosters up!"
To work at nine, and home for lunch,
Then back to work at one;
But home by five? Well, maybe not—
"Ne'er leave a job 'til done."
The town could set its clocks by him,
I've oft heard townsfolk say,
And, yet, the irony of it all
Comes back to me today—
The watch I thought was keeping time
Was ticking it away.

Reuniting After 50 Years

With few exceptions, most people would like, if at all possible, to attend their fiftieth high school reunion, if for no other reason than to satisfy a very human need to see how others have held up for so many years. At its worst, such a get-together can be dull. But at its best, it can be a thoroughly enjoyable way to catch up on one another and revive old friendships.

Well, I attended mine. I wouldn't have missed it. Not even a 900-mile drive (round trip) from the southeast corner to the northwest tip of Wisconsin along with the cost of two nights' lodging in a motel could dissuade me. I was going, and with every intention of enjoying myself.

You see, in all those fifty years, my high school had never held a reunion. During that time, no one had volunteered to organize one. But that deficiency only heightened anticipation and made the

lure of the reunion more irresistible. I had seen a few of my classmates since graduation, but in most cases a full fifty years had elapsed.

My high school, Superior Central, was located in Superior, Wisconsin. I say *was* because it does not exist any longer—although the building remains, it functions today as a junior high school. In its heyday, though, Superior Central was a famous high school.

In 1927, when I was a junior, all 1,200 pupils walked out in the first major school strike in the country. The new school superintendent had fired a beloved teacher for not changing her curriculum to suit him. When our respected principal supported the teacher, he was also fired.

The strike lasted a month and attracted reporters from *The New York Times* and other major newspapers as well as the wire services. (Had it happened today, we would probably have been on national television.) Our parents supported us, and, in the end, the superintendent and all the members of the school board were replaced. To the students' credit, the strike had been orderly, and we made up for lost time by going to school on Saturdays.

Before the strike, I had been elected prom king. Since we gave up the prom along with our Saturdays, I had the distinction of being the only prom king of Superior Central who never had a prom. But I wasn't extremely concerned; I hadn't wanted to be prom king in the first place.

Following my senior year, in 1928, President Calvin Coolidge decided to spend the summer fishing on the Brule River near Superior. He turned our high school into his summer White House. Every morning the President was driven in from the Brule, with such visiting dignitaries as Herbert Hoover, to conduct the nation's business at the school. Again national correspondents flocked to Superior. Curiously, neither of these two notable events was ever mentioned at the reunion.

The first night of the reunion, we gathered in the hall of a local steak house and received name tags. It was a bit comical that we spent the first part of the evening squinting through our bifocals at these tags; but once reacquainted, we never stopped talking.

The second evening we held our official reunion dinner in the same restaurant. Dressed in our "Sunday-go-to-meeting clothes," as we used to say, we enjoyed cocktails, a fine dinner and a brief program and danced to music provided by a small band. But as on the first night, we spent the majority of our time talking . . . but not about what we had accomplished in the world by way of occupation or financial success . . . and not about our roles as parents and grandparents . . . and not about the joys and tragedies of our lives over the past fifty years.

Then what did we talk about? We talked about the past—school days, old sweethearts, former teachers, favorite classes. I was delighted that most people remembered my father, a teacher at the school, as a great guy. In fact, one fellow named Henry Hulter recalled, "I had this Model T Ford. Gee, I was proud of that car. One day your father gave up his lunch hour to come out and paint some lines on my Model T. I'll never forget that."

I won't forget it either. I had a Model T, too. But instead of lines, Henry and I had painted messages on my car, really witty ones like, "Capacity—5

Gals," and "Don't laugh, lady, your daughter may be in this car." We wore yellow slickers in those days and painted wisecracks all over them, too. We even wore one-dollar crusher hats. Mine was purple. The entire reunion was taken up with such reminiscing.

Surprisingly, after fifty years, about one hundred former pupils showed up. With spouses, that made a total of almost two hundred. The good ladies who had organized the whole event had compiled a little booklet with the names and addresses of fellow students. It was remarkably complete. One sad note, however, was a rather long list of classmates who were no longer living. I did not know that some of them had died, including, I thought wistfully, some of the prettiest girls in the class.

The remarkable highlight of the reunion was the attendance of three former teachers. One was ninety years old. But although she was brought in from a nursing home, she was very alert and animated. I could only guess the thoughts that ran through her mind that night. The other two teachers had married since I left school, and they looked as fit as ever.

That brings me to another subject. Since my wife could not come up north with me, upon my return she asked quite naturally, "What did the women look like?"

All I could think of to say was, "Well, they all looked alike to me. They all looked fine, they all had gray hair, and they all wore flowered dresses. I really couldn't tell one from the other." That certainly wasn't true during school days.

"And what did the men look like?"

"They were gray, too, except the ones who were bald. Most of us were a bit paunchy. One old friend, who used to bang me with his elbows in basketball, had to be helped because of a stroke he had suffered."

Most of us had held up well through the years. Though many had remained in Superior, the majority had left to seek broader horizons. But all of us shared the conditioning of a childhood spent in a rugged town with a severe climate.

To sum up my reactions to the reunion, the following will suffice:

Near the end of the reunion, one committeewoman asked, "When do you think we should have another reunion?"

"How about two weeks from now?" I replied. My answer was not entirely facetious; everyone else felt the same.

Ray McBride

The story of trunks is the story of man and of his inventiveness applied to fill a need. In early times the skins of animals may have been used to hold together treasured things. The satchel, from the Greek *sakkos*, meaning a sack or bag, is of ancient vintage. Shakespeare mentions the satchel and also the trunk in his writing. Another early type of carry-all, the grip-sack, gets its name from the fact that it can be gripped in the hand.

Trunks, as we know them, may have been fashioned after the crude wooden chests which were such a necessity in early homes. It not only was a

Old Trunks
Now Collector's Item

Ethel Bruce

with animal skin, and strengthened by iron strips. Horse hide, tanned with the hair on, served as a very substantial covering for trunks of the last century. Bright brass tacks supplied an ornamental touch.

The manufacture of trunks was big business in France as early as 1596 and in London by 1763. In 1785 trunks were being made in New York. In 1860 there were 265 establishments in the United States that employed 2,092 persons making trunks. In 1893 a manufacturer of trunks and traveling bags at St. Louis carried the most common trunks, the camel back, barrel top, and flat top. One could choose between forty-two styles with outer cover in a choice of canvas, metal, enamel, duck, imitation leather veneer or sole leather. The most popular style was the 24- to 36-inch size with a lift-out tray.

storage place but served as a table or a baby bed. When the family moved to another location, the trunk or chest protected the most valuable and prized possessions during the journey. These heavy trunks are often seen in museums tied with ropes to the back of covered wagons.

What stories some trunks could tell of the wagon trains westward! Early settlers to America brought with them beautiful chests. Some were made of cypress wood, others of olive wood with panels of cedar stained to imitate mahogany. Chests from Italy were painted and gilded, those from Holland were adorned with figures of Love, Hope and Charity, and the chests of Pennsylvania Germans were often decorated in Bavarian fashion with carved ornaments, inscriptions and initials of the owner. As young ladies prepared for marriage—and they started to prepare early—these chests or trunks were filled with linens and hand-sewn items for their future homes.

Whether the family moved by boat or raft on the river, by covered wagon or, later, by train, the chest had to be sturdy to withstand travel and rugged wear. Some were constructed of wood covered

Prices for the trunks were as varied as the styles and sizes. A lady's 36-inch trunk of sole leather, linen-lined, with steel springs, would cost $31.75; with a set-up tray and adjustable hat box, parasol box and glove box the cost would climb to $44. For most, it was the sturdy, metal-covered, iron-bottomed, extra high and wide, 36-inch trunk, that sold for the bargain price of $5.95. This trunk is described as having hardwood reverse slats on top, front and ends; iron corner bumpers; patent buckle bolts; heavy hinges and valence locks; center clamps on top; cabinet lock; stitched sliding handles; large, covered, hinged tray, with bonnet box; parasol case and side compartment; fall-in-top and all-cloth facing.

Old trunks, once necessities, have become expensive collector's items. Thanks to booklets now available on the restoration of old trunks, one can turn them into useful and beautiful things. Chances are, restored trunks will be put to use storing treasured linens, blankets and quilts, just as our grandmothers' were in those earlier, simpler days.

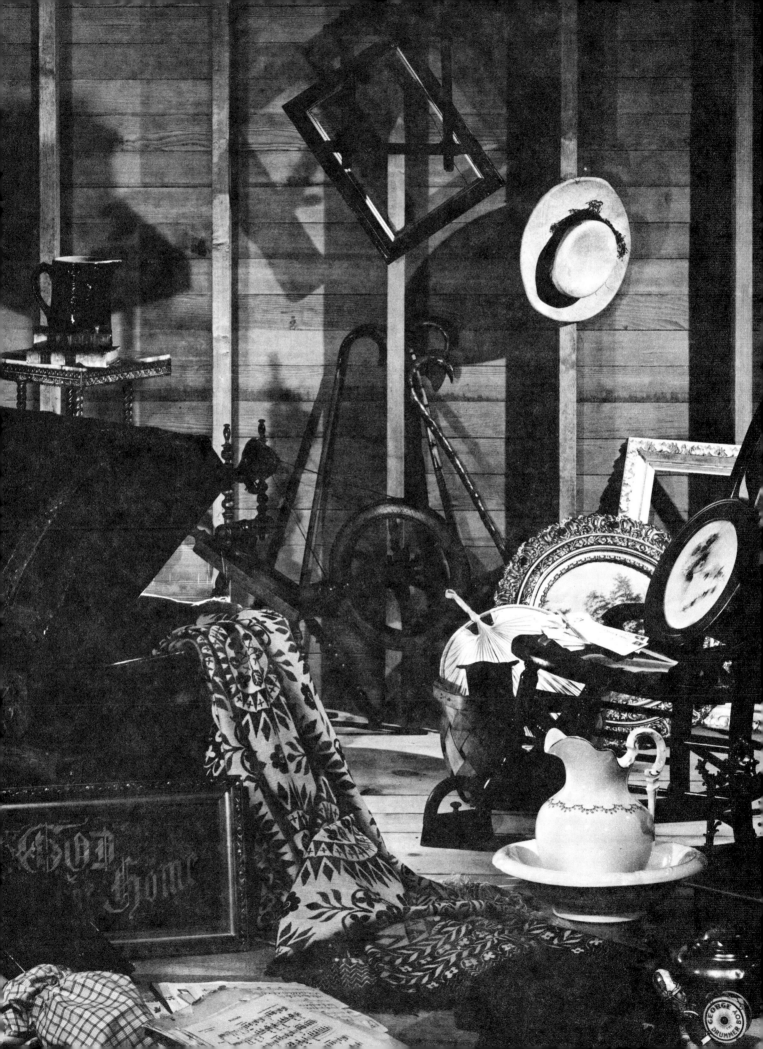

We all know that a long line of ancestors came before us. Most families have passed along stories of exceptional or endearing characters in their past. Yet, true knowledge of our families often does not go beyond those relatives we actually know. Few of us have even had the opportunity to know our great-grandparents.

Today many people's interest in their ancestry has been sparked by a desire to learn the truth behind oral traditions which have persisted in their families for generations. Did they really descend from royalty? Who was the gallant forefather who fought bravely in the Revolutionary War? For others the search is motivated by a great desire to gain a deeper understanding of who they are and where they came from.

Climbing the Family Tree

The search for one's ancestry can be approached in two basic ways. A strictly genealogical quest only reconstructs a person's line of descent. On the other hand, the work of a family historian uncovers a family line in a broader and more detailed fashion. Such research entails more than just compiling a list of names, dates and places. A family historian seeks deeper insights into the personalities and lives of ancestors.

Even before the invention of writing, many cultures passed on family histories through an oral tradition. One of the oldest written genealogical records—the "begats"— appears in the First Book of Chronicles in the Old Testament, naming Adam and Eve as the parents of the human race. In the Orient, the religious custom of ancestor worship still persists today. In our own country, Mormons, members of the Church of Jesus Christ of the Latter-Day Saints, seal the names of their ancestors in the Tabernacle, since they believe that the family is a sacred unit throughout eternity.

Uncovering the story of one's own origins is similar to doing the detective work required to solve a mystery. First, assemble the facts already known by beginning the research with the immediate family and working backward to the unknown. The first people to talk to would be relatives, especially those who are older. Take notes on the information they reveal about the family, such as names, relationships, dates of birth and death, residences and so on. Ask grandparents about what they can remember. They will probably be very pleased to talk about what happened in "the olden days."

Family reunions provide another good place to accumulate information. Whether they are small gatherings or large meetings, family reunions can be important links between generations. Family members of all ages should be included, so that young children are able to hear, first-hand, stories about their ancestors and one day pass the same anecdotes down to their own offspring.

To continue the search, look for documents and heirlooms. Relatives might well possess very detailed records. Ask to see family Bibles in which many generations of births, deaths and marriages have been recorded; examine old portraits and photograph albums to discover resemblances; study boxes of miscellaneous papers, and read diaries and letters to uncover private experiences and feelings. Inscriptions on jewelry and silver may reveal the names of ancestors and important dates in their lives.

Next, visit libraries and historical societies to study old maps and histories of the areas where forebears lived, gather any information published about branches of the family, and look through indexes of old newspapers for accounts of their lives. Once a person has discovered where his ancestors lived, he can send for copies of their birth, death and marriage certificates, visit the cemeteries in which they are buried, and search through records in county courthouses for deeds and wills.

It might even be possible to uncover the name of an ancestor who came to this country from abroad. To follow the line back to an ancestral homeland, study admission documents such as ship passenger lists and naturalization papers. At this point, either conduct research by mail or travel abroad and try to locate surviving records of the family. Since our country is made up of many different nationalities who have merged, most Americans will find that their lineage encompasses many heritages.

Most modern psychologists agree that discovering one's heritage has many benefits. A person who learns more about his family's past, their accomplishments, patterns of thinking, values, prevailing expectations and sentiments, is likely to have a better understanding of self and a clearer direction in life. It is a sense of belonging to past, present and future generations of a family unit which gives one a feeling of continuity and that special sense of identity so many people are seeking in today's society.

Michele Arrieh

I Remember Grandma!

"Pity the child who's never known
A grandmother he could call his own!"

Yes, I remember Grandma in many special ways! Particularly, I remember the hot summer days when she hovered over Grandpa just as her hens would protect their broods of scampering chicks.

From the moment he opened the patched screen door and stepped inside her domain, the bare, polished floors showed one she was in full command of about everything under her wings. "Pap," she would say in mothering tones, "Thee had better set a spell!" As he swiped his sweating brow with his chambray shirt sleeve, she would loosen his damp galluses (suspenders to you), lead him to his favorite rocker, then bustle off to ladle him a fresh, cool drink from the community dipper.

The moment he began to snooze, she waltzed back to her work, swishing her triple-skirts in that modern-day fashion. Her kitchen duties appeared endless! She ladled the jersey cream, patted the golden nuggets, spanked the shiny, raw loaves in expert fashion, scoured the buckeye brown floors, shooed hungry flies with her apron, and captured summer into jellies and preserves.

Oh, the jelly my grandmother poured was as manna from heaven. It boasted an upright stance and an undiluted flavor—quite different from the anemic product prepared today. It refused to slump when inverted into her glass jelly dish, the one with the six-inch foot. That jelly dish is resting in my kitchen today.

Her jelly and gingersnaps made her famous among her family of descendants. And that was a big family! She kept the filled glasses high out of reach, but her chewy snaps rested in a gray stone cookie jar on the lower pantry shelf. They fairly oozed with ginger but they were not off limits to visiting grandchildren. I ought to know. And she always left the lid loosely fitting.

I loved to watch her at her tasks, especially as she skimmed the gravy-cream off the day-old milk. She always pushed her right forefinger around the inside top to glean every molecule. To be certain none were wasted she licked that finger in smacking-fashion. Then on to the next crock to repeat the process.

Now, she had the "well" room right next to her kitchen. There was a water pump here, and a long wooden trough such as Grandpa always used to water the stock. Here the crocks of milk would be set in the cold water for cream to "rise."

If she were churning I relished a glass of buttermilk after every last nugget had been gleaned from her wooden churn. I remember how deftly she wielded the slightly palmed butter paddle which Grandpap had hewn and polished. Probably made from apple or ash; no one seems to remember.

Though her larder was well-stocked, her medicine cupboard, had she owned one, would have remained as empty as Old Mother Hubbard's.

Not many would recognize her prescriptions for soothing lotions, medicinal applications or her sick remedies. I would never think of funneling a sheet of writing "ink" paper and lighting it, holding it over a saucer to catch the iodine for treating ringworm. Neither would I use jersey cream for a facial, kerosene to ease a sore throat, warm castor oil for an earache. She often used raspberry leaf tea for diarrhea, or a pinch of plug tobacco to quiet an empty, quaking tooth.

Yes, Grandmother used many of these methods to rear her brood of nine to adulthood. One particular antidote was kept in the woodshed! Father assures me it was always handy and in a limber condition. I never became acquainted with this particular application, but her other remedies were in heavy demand.

I cannot remember Grandmother ever being ill, nor even slightly indisposed. Nor did I ever see her "catnap" as Grandpap did. Her hands seemed never to know idleness. . . .

I could never forget the day her kitchen cabinet was moved the quarter mile to our house! There it stood against the west kitchen wall. There were small-doored sections for spices; four long, narrow drawers for odds and ends; a bread board which pulled out when needed. There were a cutlery drawer, a drawer for recipes, and one long opening which held the flour sifter and twenty-five pounds of flour.

Two huge, cradle-type bins, one for cornmeal and one for forty-nine pounds of flour left room for the big flour scoop. These bins sat next to the floor, just as those pictured in 1900 catalogs.

One could not measure our surprise when Father lifted the two bins out for a sun airing. And there, on a secret shelf to the back of the cabinet sat a wholly unexpected cache of Grandmother's jelly. It was craftily hidden, no doubt for a purpose. Each jelly glass, when emptied, we found decorated in the bottom with a goodluck horseshoe! Today, these are collectors' items.

The memory of all that delicacy which neither Mother nor sister could make because of the expense of the sugar, was too vivid to be forgotten!

Yes, I remember Grandma in a pleasant way!

Ellen Rebecca (Mills) Fenn

Hansel and Gretel

by Jakob and Wilhelm Grimm

A fairy tale to be shared and enjoyed by all ages.

Once upon a time there dwelt near a large wood a poor woodcutter, with his wife and two children by his former marriage, a little boy called Hansel, and a girl named Gretel. He had little enough work to do, and once, when there was a great famine in the land, he could not procure even his daily bread. As he lay thinking in his bed one evening, he sighed and said to his wife, "What will become of us? How can we feed our children when we have no more than we can eat ourselves?"

"Know then, my husband," answered she, "we will lead them away quite early in the morning into the thickest part of the wood and there make them a fire and give them each a little piece of bread; then we will go to our work and leave them alone. They will not find the way home again, and we shall be freed from them."

"No, Wife," replied he, "that I can never do. How can you bring your heart to leave my children all alone in the wood, for the wild beasts will soon come and tear them to pieces?"

"Oh, you simpleton!" said she. "Then we must all four die of hunger." But she left him no peace till he consented, saying, "Ah, but I shall miss the poor children."

The two children, however, had not gone to sleep since they were so hungry, and so they overheard what the stepmother said to their father. Gretel wept bitterly and said to Hansel, "What will become of us?"

"Be quiet, Gretel," said he. "Do not cry—I will soon help you."

And as soon as their parents had fallen asleep, he got up, put on his coat, and unbarring the back door, slipped out. The moon shone brightly and the white pebbles which lay before the door seemed like silver pieces, they glittered so brightly. Hansel stooped down and put as many into his pocket as it would hold, and then going back he said to Gretel, "Be comforted, dear sister, and sleep in peace; God will not forsake us." And so saying, he went to bed again.

The next morning, before the sun arose, the wife went and awoke the two children. "Get up, you lazy things; we are going into the forest to chop wood." Then she gave them each a piece of bread, saying,

"There is something for your dinner. Do not eat it before the time, for you will get nothing else." Gretel took the bread in her apron, for Hansel's pocket was full of pebbles, and so they all set out upon their way.

When they had gone a little distance Hansel stood still and peeped back at the house; and this he repeated several times, till his father said, "Hansel, what are you peeping at, and why do you lag behind? Take care, and remember your legs."

"Ah, Father," said Hansel, "I am looking at my white cat sitting upon the roof of the house and trying to say good-bye."

"You simpleton!" said the wife. "That is not a cat, it is only the sun shining on the white chimney."

But in reality Hansel was not looking at a cat. Every time he stopped, he dropped a pebble out of his pocket upon the path.

When they came to the middle of the wood the father told the children to collect wood and he would make them a fire so that they would not be cold. So Hansel and Gretel gathered together quite a little mountain of twigs. Then they set fire to them, and as the flame burnt up high the wife said, "Now you children, lie down near the fire and rest yourselves, while we go into the forest and chop wood. When we are ready, I will come and call you."

Hansel and Gretel sat down by the fire, and when it was noon, each ate the piece of bread, and because they could hear the blows of an axe they thought their father was near. But it was not an axe, but a branch which he had bound to a withered tree, so as to be blown to and fro by the wind. They waited so long that at last their eyes closed from weariness and they fell fast asleep.

When they awoke it was quite dark and Gretel began to cry. "How shall we get out of the wood?"

But Hansel tried to comfort her by saying, "Wait, a little while till the moon rises and then we will quickly find the way."

The moon soon shone forth, and Hansel, taking his sister's hand, followed the pebbles, which glittered like new-coined silver pieces, and showed them the path. All night long they walked on, and as day broke they came to their father's house. They knocked at the door, and when the wife opened it and saw Hansel and Gretel she exclaimed, "You wicked children! Why did you sleep so long in the wood? We thought you were never coming home again." But their father was very glad, for it had grieved his heart to leave them all alone.

Not long afterwards there was again great scarcity in every corner of the land, and one night

continued

the children overheard their mother saying to their father, "Everything is again consumed. We have only half a loaf left and then the song is ended. The children must be sent away. We will take them deeper into the wood so that they may not find the way out again. It is the only escape for us."

But her husband felt heavy at heart and thought, "It would be better to share the last crust with the children." His wife, however, would listen to nothing that he said, and scolded and reproached him without end.

The children, however, had heard the conversation as they lay awake. As soon as the old people went to sleep Hansel got up, intending to pick up some pebbles as before, but the wife had locked the door so that he could not get out. Nevertheless, he comforted Gretel, saying, "Do not cry, sleep in quiet, the good God will not forsake us."

Early in the morning the stepmother came and pulled them out of bed and gave them each a slice of bread which was still smaller than the former piece. On the way, Hansel broke his in his pocket and, stooping every now and then, dropped a crumb upon the path.

The mother led the children deep into the wood where they had never been before, and there, making an immense fire, she said to them, "Sit down here and rest, and when you feel tired you can sleep for a little while. We are going into the forest to hew wood, and in the evening, when we are ready, we will come and fetch you."

When noon came Gretel shared her bread with Hansel, who had strewn his on the path. Then they went to sleep, but the evening arrived and no one came to visit the poor children. In the dark night they awoke and Hansel comforted his sister by saying, "Only wait, Gretel, till the moon comes out, then we shall see the crumbs of bread which I have dropped and they will show us the way home."

The moon shone and they got up, but they could not see any crumbs, for the thousands of birds which had been flying about in the woods and fields had picked them all up.

They walked the whole night long and the next day, but even then they did not come out of the wood; and they got so hungry, for they had nothing to eat but the berries which they found upon the bushes. Soon they got so tired that they could not drag themselves along, so they lay down under a tree and went to sleep.

It was now the third morning since they had left their father's house and they still walked on; but they only got deeper and deeper into the wood, and Hansel saw that if help did not come very soon they would die of hunger. As soon as it was noon they saw, sitting upon a bough, a beautiful snow-white bird, which sang so sweetly that they stood still and listened to it. It soon stopped singing, and, spreading its wings, flew away. They followed it until it arrived at a cottage, where it perched upon the roof. And when they went close up to it they saw that the cottage was made of bread and cakes, and the windowpanes were of clear sugar.

"We will go in here," said Hansel, "and have a glorious feast. I will eat a piece of the roof and you can eat the window. Will they not be sweet?" So Hansel reached up and broke a piece off the roof in order to see how it tasted, while Gretel stepped up to the window and began to bite it.

Just then the door opened and a very old woman, walking upon crutches, came out. Hansel and Gretel were so frightened that they let fall what they had in their hands; but the old woman, nodding her head, said, "Ah, you dear children, what has brought you here? Come in and stop with me and no harm shall befall you"; and so saying she took them both by the hand and led them into her cottage. A good meal of milk and pancakes, with sugar, apples and nuts, was spread on the table.

In the back room were two nice little beds, covered with white, where Hansel and Gretel laid themselves down and thought themselves in heaven. The old woman behaved very kindly to them, but in reality she was a wicked witch who waylaid children. She built the bread house in order to entice them in; but as soon as they were in her power she killed them, cooked and ate them, and made a great festival of the day.

Witches have red eyes and cannot see very far, but they have a fine sense of smell, like wild beasts, so that they know when children approach them. When Hansel and Gretel came near the witch's house she laughed wickedly, saying, "Here come two who shall not escape me." And early in the morning, before they awoke, she went up to them and saw how lovingly they lay sleeping, with their chubby, red cheeks, and she mumbled to herself, "That will be a good bite." Then she took up Hansel with her rough hand and shut him up in a little cage with a lattice door; and, although he screamed loudly, it was of no use. Gretel came next, and, shaking her till she awoke, she said, "Get up, you lazy thing, and fetch some water to cook something good for your brother, who must remain in that stall and get fat. When he is fat enough I shall eat him." Gretel began to cry, but it was useless, for the old witch made her do as she wished. So a nice meal was cooked for Hansel, but Gretel got nothing but a crab's claw.

Every morning the old witch came to the cage and said, "Hansel, stretch out your finger that I may feel whether you are getting fat." But Hansel would stretch out a bone, and the old woman, having very bad sight, thought it was his finger, and wondered very much that he did not get more fat. When four weeks had passed and Hansel still kept quite lean, she lost all her patience and would not wait any longer.

"Gretel," she called out in a passion, "get some water quickly; be Hansel fat or lean, this morning I will kill and cook him."

Oh, how the poor little sister grieved, as she was forced to fetch the water, and fast the tears ran down her cheeks! "Dear, good God, help us now!" she exclaimed.

But the old witch called out, "Leave off that noise. It will not help you a bit."

So early in the morning Gretel was forced to go out and fill the kettle and make a fire. "First we will bake, however," said the old woman. "I have already heated the oven and kneaded the dough," and so saying, she pushed poor Gretel up to the oven, out of which the flames were burning fiercely. "Creep in," said the witch, "and see if it is hot enough and then we will put in the bread." But she intended when Gretel got in to shut up the oven and let her bake, so that she might eat her as well as Hansel.

Gretel perceived what her thoughts were and said, "I do not know how to do it; how shall I get in?"

"You stupid goose," said she, "the opening is big enough. See, I could even get in myself!" And she got up and put her head into the oven. Then Gretel gave her a push, so that she fell right in, and then, shutting the iron door, she bolted it. Oh! How horribly she howled, but Gretel ran away and left the ungodly witch to burn to ashes.

Now she ran to Hansel and, opening his door, called out, "Hansel, we are saved; the old witch is dead!"

And now, as there was nothing to fear, they went into the witch's house, where in every corner were chests full of pearls and precious stones. "These are better than pebbles," said Hansel, putting as many into his pocket as it would hold, while Gretel thought, "I will take some home, too," and filled her apron full.

"We must be off now," said Hansel, "and get out of this enchanted forest." But when they had walked for two hours they came to a large lake.

"We cannot get over," said Hansel. "I can see no bridge at all."

"And there is no boat either," said Gretel, "but there swims a white duck, I will ask her to help us over," and she sang:

"Little duck, good little duck,
    Gretel and Hansel, here we stand;
There is neither stile nor bridge,
    Take us on your back to land."

So the duck came to them, and Hansel sat himself on and bade his sister sit behind him.

"No," answered Gretel, "that will be too much for the duck. She shall take us over one at a time." This the good little bird did, and when both were happily arrived on the other side, and had gone a little way, they came to a well-known wood, which they knew better every step they went, and at last they perceived their father's house.

Then they began to run, and, bursting into the house, they fell on their father's neck. He had not had one happy hour since he had left the children in the forest, and his wife was dead. Gretel shook her apron and the pearls and precious stones rolled out upon the floor, and Hansel threw down one handful after the other out of his pocket. Then all their sorrows were ended and they lived happily ever after.

Grandfather Recalls
the Dwarf of the Baseball Diamond

I remember my first practice with his school.
He stuck his glove on the wrong hand and—
after I'd just corrected three kids for the
same mistake—tried to bat cross-handed.
About a week later an easy fly ball
dropped through his hands and clipped him
square on the forehead. But he blinked back
most of his tears and refused to leave the game.
I ruffled his hair and he spun away, embarrassed,
determination glinting in his moist eyes.
That was just over a year ago.
He's grown a bit, but so have the
other boys, and my favorite second baseman
is still usually the dwarf of the diamond.
His team played yesterday. He led off the game by
taking a called strike three that was almost
in the dirt, but after a quick, unbelieving glance
at the umpire he hustled back to the bench.
He cracked a double over third base in his second at-bat.
The next time up he caught the third baseman
playing deep and laid down a perfect bunt for
another hit, the first time I'd seen him dare to try
in a game the play we'd practiced so many hours.
There wasn't even a throw to first.
His teammates yelled their approval, and
he grinned like the sun as he waved
to me, keeping score on the sidelines.
I saluted with clenched fist as something
welled up for both of us, spilling over,
but anybody looking my way
would have thought I, shielded by my sunglasses,
was just wiping some sweat off my face.

                                    Tom Hazuka

CAROLE BOERKE

What Grandchildren Do

Edgar A. Guest

This is what a grandchild does:
  Brushes off the years;
Polishes a grandpa's smiles,
  Banishes his fears;
Lightens up his step a bit; brings
  Him tasks to do;
Teaches him to play once more
  Games which once he knew.
Leads him to the candy shops, in
  His world of men,
Sends him on his daily round
  Young at heart again.

Grandfolks have no time to think
  They are getting old.
They must learn anew the rhymes
  And the tales they told.
They must plan for circus time,
  Wander round the zoo;
Call the animals by name, as they
  Used to do.
They've no voice for aches and
  Pains. Young at heart are they.
Eastertide is theirs once more, and
  The Christmas Day!

This is what a grandchild does:
  Long-lost joys restores;
Gives age back the birds and
  Flowers and the out-of-doors;
Pleasures lost and long forgot;
  Songs it used to sing;
Princes in the golden towers;
  Butterflies a-wing;
Every charm that childhood bears
  In its joyous train,
For a third time down the years . . .
  All is ours again!

The Road
to Grandmother's

Ah, me, for the road that led away
Between the rows of the hedges tall,
With a stretch of haze low down in the west,
And a shimmer of clouds high over all.
And there were the fields of dreaming wheat
With a lark a-singing low in the grass,
With never a fear and never a care
For the passing by of a little lass.
And there was the breath of the clover blooms,
And the berry brambles a-reaching far,
But not so far as the heart of me
Reaching out where the dream worlds are.

And the road to Grandmother's led away
Straight on and on 'til it came to the sea,
With the white waves curling out in the bay,
And always a ship waiting there for me.
And I never knew to be tired then,
Nor weary at all when the day was done,
And I'd walk the road from Grandmother's home,
Blithe and gay at the set of sun.
Ah, the road in the morning was glad and fair,
But at night the light from the early star
Was a white ship bearing me home again
From the far countries where the dream worlds are.

And there was my own mother awaiting me,
All tender and sweet in the front yard grass,
And there was a bed snug up to the eaves
Willing to welcome a little lass.
But now, ah, me, I'm tired at night,
And the road would be all too weary and long,
And my heart does not lift as it used to do
At hearing the trill of a wild bird's song,
And there'd be nobody waiting my coming home . . .
But remembering of it is good and sweet.
Dear God, please make me to know again
The feel of the old road to my feet.

Grace Noll Crowell

"The Road to Grandmother's" from *Bright Harvest* by Grace Noll Crowell. Copyright 1952 by Harper & Row, Publishers, Inc. Reprinted by permission of the publisher.

The Zehnder Kissing Bridge

"Daddy is the only grandfather I know of who carries pictures of covered bridges instead of his grandchildren," wrote Isabel Graton-Dittrich in the preface to her father's book, *The Last of the Covered Bridge Builders.* Now nearing completion, the last of the covered bridges, built by the last of the covered bridge builders, spans the Cass River in the heart of Frankenmuth, Michigan.

The Zehnder Holz-Brucke (wooden bridge), an authentic 239-foot replica of a nineteenth century bridge, is the dream of two brothers, Edwin and William Zehnder, brought to reality by Milton S. Graton of Ashland, New Hampshire.

Feeling the need for additional parking space for their own prestigious restaurants and for other establishments in the area, the brothers looked across the river, which at this point flowed parallel to the main street. After purchasing land on the east bank—enough acreage to accommodate 250 cars and fifty buses—they turned their attention to the problems of having a bridge constructed to carry traffic across the river. Just any kind of concrete and steel bridge would not do. It had to conform to the character of this German town with its old-world Bavarian architecture.

In 1973, William Zehnder read an article on covered wooden bridges in *Grit* magazine, in which Milton S. Graton was recognized as the "foremost authority on and builder of covered bridges in this country." Mr. Zehnder immediately

made contact with the man. Official red tape proved to be an almost insurmountable obstacle; but on April 20, 1978, a handwritten contract was drawn up between the Zehnder family and Graton Associates.

Milton S. Graton is devoted to the restoration of old "kissing bridges," reflecting the romance of the past when couples "cuddled in their buggies hidden from the eyes of nosey neighbors." He was the perfect choice to build the bridge for Frankenmuth, "a village dedicated to the preservation of the Old-Country way of life."

Graton refers to a completed bridge as "one of our children." When asked why he was willing to come to Michigan—so far from home—to build a bridge, when he and his son have a flourishing business in New England, his answer was, "The Zehnder family wanted a bridge here, and so we came and visited them and looked over their real estate, and we noticed it was very well cared for. So it would be fair to assume that if we built them a bridge, the bridge would be taken care of after we went home. That's why we're here working a thousand miles from home." He says the Zehnder Holz-Brucke is a five-hundred-year proposition" if is it cared for.

Construction, which began in the spring of 1979, did not start in Frankenmuth as one might expect, but rather in the Graton warehouse in Ashland, where Milton, age seventy, and his son

Arnold, forty-two, fashioned the roof rafters, made the trunnels and planed trim boards. These components were then shipped to Frankenmuth, where the remainder of the work is being done.

Mr. Graton brought some of the lumber from New Hampshire, and three train car loads of Douglas Fir were shipped in from Oregon. However, he faced the problem of acquiring lumber for the shingles, which he said had to be made of cedar. After driving a thousand miles throughout Michigan's heavily-forested Upper Peninsula in search of white cedar, Mr. Graton and his wife returned to Frankenmuth discouraged, for they had found none at all. However, news traveled "by the grapevine" that cedar was needed for the Frankenmuth bridge, reaching a man in the Alpena area who was in the process of timbering off sixty-five acres, in the center of which lay a swamp nurturing a stand of cedar trees. A deal for the trees was soon consummated.

Mr. Graton was delighted to find that in the friendly town of Frankenmuth many people volunteered to help in any way they could. Making the shingles was a job they could do without training. Six to eight friends of the project, all retirees, under the supervision of a retired "master mechanic," spent seventy-five days cutting sixty-two thousand board feet of cedar, spruce, and Norway pine for the shingles and decking for the bridge. On being asked when he planned to retire from retirement, this supervisor commented, "We work hard because we don't have to!"

Every shingle was marked so that when it was placed on the roof, it would lie "heart side out"—that is, so that the side of the shingle that had faced the interior of the tree would be exposed to the weather. If the shingle were to curl, it would curl outward. The shingles were then placed so that the grain in the wood ran in the direction that would shed water.

The town lattice work on the bridge is both attractive and sturdy. The design of criss-crossing planks was named for its originator, Ithiel Town. Planks are placed in this pattern and fastened together with trunnels (a combination of the two words *tree nails*) which are about two feet in length. Mr. Graton figures that a hole for a trunnel is the right size if he can drive the trunnel into the hole one inch with one blow of a sixteen-pound sledge hammer.

According to Mr. Graton, "When you're building something, you pound a board on, then you stand back and look at it, and if it doesn't look right, you go pound it off and put it on a little differently—architectural drawing or no."

And so at last, the bridge, meticulously constructed (on the east bank) in the way such bridges were built in early America, was ready to be moved into place on the pilings built in the river to support it. The process required twelve days—January 18 through January 29—with action scheduled for two hours in the morning and two in the afternoon. Camera fans and thousands of curious onlookers swarmed into Frankenmuth to watch the bridge being pulled down the incline of the river bank, onto tracks laid for it, and into place across the river.

The 230-ton structure was moved in the old-fashioned way, utilizing a system of block, capstan, come-alongs and pulleys that enabled each of two oxen to pull as much as 180 oxen could normally displace. Two teams of oxen provided the pulling power. One team didn't seem to relish the idea of walking in a circle for an extended period of time around the capstan; however, the other team "stole the show" as they proudly—even gracefully—followed the circular path as though they were responsible for the whole thing.

Zehnder's Holz-Brucke is a masterpiece of craftsmanship, designed to complement the surroundings. Gables and dormer windows in the roof blend with the Bavarian architecture. Some finishing work remains to be done; but the bridge will be open for traffic sometime during the summer and will be dedicated in September.

Mr. Graton says he derives such great satisfaction from what he is doing he will continue the work he has engaged in for fifty years, as long as he retains his health. To him it makes no sense "to pay out money to play golf, just to be doing something; I might as well be pounding trunnels as playing a golf ball. This way I can see where I hit."

Charles Kuralt of CBS News wrote in a foreword to Graton's book, "In an age in which we do so many things fast and wrong, Milton Graton does things slowly and right. He is the equal of the great craftsmen of our past and, we may hope, a strong link in a chain of craftsmanship which will never quite die out in America."

As someone has said, "A covered bridge is more than just timber and trunnels. A covered bridge is a masterpiece of one generation to endure for the pleasure of another!" The Zehnder Holz-Brucke in Frankenmuth is such a masterpiece.

Doris A. Paul

The Water Mill

Sarah Doudney

Listen to the water mill,
Through the livelong day;
How the clicking of the wheel
Wears the hours away.

Languidly the autumn wind
Stirs the withered leaves;
On the field the reapers sing,
Binding up the sheaves;
And a proverb haunts my mind,
And as a spell is cast,
"The mill will never grind
With the water that has passed."

Autumn winds revive no more
Leaves strewn o'er earth and main.
The sickle never more shall reap
The yellow, garnered grain;

And the rippling stream flows on
Tranquil, deep and still,
Never gliding back again
To the water mill.
Truly speaks the proverb old,
With a meaning vast:
"The mill will never grind
With the water that has passed."

Work, while yet the sun does shine,
Men of strength and will!
Never does the streamlet glide
Useless by the mill.

Wait not till tomorrow's sun
Beams brightly on thy way;
All that thou canst call thine own
Lies in this word: "Today!"
Power, intellect and health
Will not always last:
"The mill will never grind
With the water that has passed."

. . .

. . . Leave no tender word unsaid,
But love while love shall last:
"The mill will never grind
With the water that has passed."

. . .

. . . Take the proverb to thy soul!
Take, and clasp it fast:
"The mill will never grind
With the water that has passed."

. . .

Pussy Willows and Hideouts

Colleen Reece

When I was a child and read fairy tales I used to sigh, wishing I had a fairy godmother who would grant me just one wish. Always my wish was different—to be rich, to be kind, to be loved—whatever appealed, according to my mood. But now as I smile at the child I once was, my imagination still sometimes asks: If I had a fairy godmother, what wish would I want granted most? Today the answer is always the same—to be allowed, if only for a moment, to go back to the days of pussy willows and hideouts. . . .

Childhood in the country. A big, old-fashioned house that was a real home. Two acres of land of our own, hundreds of acres surrounding us, owned by friends and relatives, uncleared except for houses perhaps a quarter-mile apart, or gardens here and there. A world of freedom, a world of invitation, adventure, excitement. Depending on which game we played, spies, cowboys or Indians lurked behind every giant tree, every overgrown thicket or bush. But there were times when the active games palled. Those were the times for the pussy willows and hideouts.

At the edge of our property stood a huge, gnarled pussy willow tree. The bark was worn from sturdy climbing shoes, much more so even than the swaying white birches. For high in the branches of that pussy willow tree was a seat—a natural resting place for tired children, who would climb to where the two strong branches crossed, settle down with a book and apple, and be lost to the rest of the world for a time.

In the spring that tree offered decoration for every room in the house. Branchy stalks of tiny, kitten-like, furry-gray catkins! How we waited for them! They were truly the sign spring had come, following the dark, cold, confined winter. But they were also a sign it was warm enough—with a sweater—to climb to our "seat." It would be impossible to calculate how many books my two brothers and I read there, or how many apple cores were heaved back over the fence from our high perch. Who needed television? We had our own world of imagination up there among the branches. . . .

It was there we dreamed our dreams, planned our schemes, dozed and rested, often with a purring cat in our laps, high above the common earth.

There were other hideouts, one in the huge fir stump by our sandpit. It was deliciously sticky with pitch, and smelled heavenly. There was another, halfway to the nearest neighbors, a big fir with a broad stump as part of its base. There was also the huge, old, sawdust pile. All were wonderful places to play, but none could take the place of that seat in the willow tree.

One memory stands out. It was late fall, almost early winter. Somehow, somewhere I had dropped my doll, not the big beautiful one but the small, old, worn-out companion who had been in the willow tree with me when I didn't feel like being with anyone else. Now she was gone forever. Heartbroken, I sought comfort from my tree, but its empty arms could only reach out to me in sympathy. The snows came, then melted, and from somewhere beneath their covering blanket my doll was unearthed. She was pitiful. Her face was cracked, her head torn open. Tears poured. But a skillful father restuffed her head, a loving mother made a covering cap. Only the chipped paint on her face was a silent reminder, as we once again climbed our tree, that she had lain lonely and forsaken all winter. Yet because of her scars I loved her even more. No other doll would ever usurp a small girl's love for "crack-headed Janette."

Pussy willows and hideouts. Place to play, or to be alone. Secret, secure worlds where troubles could be left behind, or sorrows eased by the songs of a hundred birds as they shared our havens.

Why the appeal of those places? Was it the security of knowing they would always be there, ready, waiting, when spring came once again? Spring, summer, fall. Early and late. Often we ran home just ahead of the darkness, sure a thousand monsters were pursuing us, falling into our parents' arms with dirty hands, empty stomachs, but contended hearts.

What if my fairy godmother really granted my wish to return? Would I find my wonderful willow to be just another old, gnarled tree? Would my hideouts be ordinary stumps and trees, and my sawdust pile old and ugly? It is probably just as well I can't go back, only to find it changed. Yet my days of pussy willows and hidehouts will never quite be over. As long as I can close my eyes and drift back in memory, my wish is granted, over and over. And every bouquet of pussy willow will return me to those long-gone days when Dad, Mom, the boys and I shared an old-fashioned home furnished with love, pussy willows and hideouts.

Vistas of Memories and Hope

Here in the firelight we sit,
A trifle weary, resting a bit—
A grateful pair who count our wealth
In vistas of memories, happiness and health.

We offer Him a twilight prayer
For all the blessings that we share:
Our devoted children, and theirs, snug in bed,
Safely housed, protected, fed.

We hope and dream that we may be
Forever united with family and Thee—
Worthily united in heaven above—
After life's work is ended in kindness and love.

Rosalie Fladoos

Painted Dreams

I've often thought how very drab
This life of ours would be,
If day by day, we went our way
And made no move to see
Our hopes and plans for years to come,
Fulfilled in visions rare;
To free our fancy, let it rise
Beyond today—for there,
Waiting for us in the future,
True happiness, it seems,
Is ours for just the taking
In precious "Painted Dreams."

A mother singing to her child,
Looks forward through the years,
And standing, straight and strong and true,
A full-grown man appears.
An honest, righteous, upright man—
A man the world admires;
Why, that's her baby when he's grown,
And mother never tires
Of looking toward the future days
And scheming little schemes,
To make her boy the man she sees
In all her "Painted Dreams."

And sweethearts since the world began
Have pushed the years away
And planned the future, step by step
Until that wondrous day—
That day when man and wife they'll be,
To face life hand in hand.
Yes, that's a vision ages old
And yet, it's no less grand
Today than it was years ago,
To see how love light gleams
And lights the way for lovers
Who follow "Painted Dreams."

Sometimes I think the old folks paint
The sweetest dreams of all,
For memories of all the years
Await their beck and call.
And somehow, time in rolling by
Erases all that's bad,
And leaves them naught but visions
Of ev'ry joy they've had.
For one sweet thought from out the past,
A world of tears redeems
To those who find their happiness
Reliving "Painted Dreams."

Author Unknown

Of "Colored Sticks" and Crayons

Audrey Carli

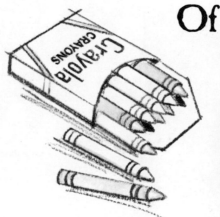

If you are a parent, you know what happiness that plain, little, colored stick called a crayon has brought to your children—especially on long, rainy days.

You know what fun it is to put the children's drawings on the family bulletin board for all to admire. You have glowed inwardly at your child's or grandchild's first crayoned picture—a house with a spider-like, yellow sun beaming down, an ordinary tree from your yard, with many branches and green leaves, or loved ones in stick-like forms. If you are a grandparent, you probably wouldn't feel your home is complete without a package of color crayons in the drawer awaiting your grandchild's visit.

But where did these small, but irreplaceable, colored sticks come from? The inventor of the crayon was a French artist named Antoine-Joseph Loriot, who was trying to create something better for drawing. And he did so at age twenty-nine in 1745.

Loriot had grown discouraged with drawing materials that smeared. So he continued to work on various kinds of drawing tools. In less than a year, Loriot had invented the first color crayon by mixing powdered colors in melted beeswax. The cooled product resembled today's crayons. He and other artists called them "colored sticks of hardened wax."

However, Loriot's excitement was short-lived. Beeswax was difficult to keep in supply. And other waxes melted too easily. Loriot's fellow artists did not like the wax sticks. They tried them, then threw them away! The dismayed Loriot did not even bother to patent his invention.

Even though other artists did not use the first color crayons in their work, the enthusiastic Loriot did. He died in 1782, still feeling the crayons were worthwhile.

He could never have foreseen that his beeswax sticks would be made from petroleum wax someday, or that they would be in art stores, variety stores and other shops. He could not have guessed that crayons would be standard supplies in elementary schools.

Yet, had he not invented his "colored sticks," how could children create those first kindergarten pictures? How could little ones give those first very personalized gifts—pictures drawn and carefully colored while visiting Grandpa and Grandma's house? How could moms survive those rainy days at home with peppy youngsters? And how could those budding artists develop their talents and receive, for those early efforts, all that loving praise from parents and grandparents?

Our gratitude to Antoine-Joseph Loriot for bringing to our lives the colors of joy.

Full moon casts an eerie glow
On the darkened streets below;
Old owls hooting,
Dry leaves scooting;
Halloween is near.

Wax and Wane

Witches, goblins, ghouls and ghosts,
Apple-bobbing, chestnut roasts;
Trick-or-treating
Candy-eating;
Halloween is here.

Sticky fingers, sticky smiles,
Candy left in sticky piles;
Tummies aching,
Wise heads shaking;
Halloween is past.

Halloween Handouts

It's that time of the year again when pint-sized monsters, toothless vampires, freckle-faced fairy princesses and charcoal-whiskered hoboes descend upon the streets in droves on their annual trick-or-treat raid. Armed with plastic swords, cap-loaded six-shooters and, of course, the essential goodie bags, they are amply prepared to make their demands on the older generations. But these tiny invaders are not without scruples; in exchange for a stick of bubble gum or a chocolate-centered sucker, the generous door-opener receives a quick over-the-shoulder "thank you" as the trick-or-treater races to the next house.

As the recipient of many of these grateful utterances, you might ask, "How did such an event ever get started in the first place?"

Good question. Well, you can blame the Celtics.

Nearly two thousand years ago, these ancient inhabitants of pre-Christian Ireland and Great Britain held their new year festival, Samhain (end of summer), on the eve of October 31. They believed that on that night the spirits of their departed kinspeople could return for the celebration. Of course, if these spirits were free for the night, so were the fairies, witches and other agents of the supernatural free—to roam the countryside and wreak mischievous havoc. In-evitably, Samhain acquired superstitious over-tones as the weak of heart began performing certain rituals to ward off these evil spirits.

"But what does that have to do with trick-or-treating?" you might wonder.

When the expansionist Romans finally subdued these Isles, they adapted many of the Celtic festivals to Christianity, including Samhain. Observing November 1 as All Saint's Day, they gave the night before religious significance designating it All Hallows Eve—hence, the name *Halloween*.

So through the centuries, Latin countries celebrated Halloween as a holy day. The Isles, on the other hand, persisted in observing their ancient rituals, eventually spreading them to the United States. One custom the Irish immigrants imported was the practice of going from house to house demanding gifts of food for the evening's festivities. This custom developed into present-day trick-or-treating.

So you see, Halloween handouts evolved from a pagan harvest festival.

This year when those little trick-or-treaters come to the door, think about the centuries of tradition they represent. On second thought, just enjoy the fun. After all, Halloween comes but once a year.

Beverly Wiersum Charette

ACKNOWLEDGMENTS

TIME'S SOUVENIR by June Masters Bacher. Previously published in *Good Old Days*. Permission granted to reprint. AUTUMN CRICKETS; AUTUMN GARDEN; GIVING; THE LAST CORN SHOCK; SEPTEMBER WATERCOLOR; WILD GEESE OVER THE DESERT by Glenn Ward Dresbach. From *The Collected Poems, 1914-1948, of Glenn Ward Dresbach* (Caxton, 1950). Some biographical data on Glenn Ward Dresbach supplied by *The Kansas City Star*. WHAT GRANDCHILDREN DO by Edgar A. Guest. Copyrighted. Used by permission. TIME IS A MEASURE . . . by Margie Lee Johnson. From *Timberline and Other Poems* by Margie Lee Johnson. Copyright © 1964 by Margie Lee Johnson. Published by Dorrance & Company. PUSSY WILLOWS AND HIDEOUTS by Colleen L. Reece. Previously published in *The Ruralite*, March 1979. A MOTHER SPEAKS by Alice Kennelly Roberts. Copyrighted. Used with permission of the author. Our sincere thanks to the following authors whose addresses we were unable to locate: Josephine Millard for GRANDMOTHERS; Ella A. Stone for UNFOLDMENT.

COLOR ART AND PHOTO CREDITS
(in order of appearance)

Front cover, Camerique; inside front cover, Colour Library International (USA) Limited; Happy couple, Four By Five, Inc.; Flower garden, Freelance Photographers Guild; Historic house in Georgetown, Colorado, Ed Cooper; Pink rose, Sister Anne Marie, G.N.S.H.; Harvesting tomatoes, Freelance Photographers Guild; Celosia, Sister Anne Marie, G.N.S.H.; Old-fashioned kitchen, Gerald Koser; A gift from Grandma, Four By Five, Inc.; A hug for Grandpa, Four By Five, Inc.; Grandma's rocking chair, Freelance Photographer's Guild; GRANDMOTHER READING TO THE CHILDREN, Mary Cassatt, Three Lions, Inc.; Gathering leaves, Freelance Photographers Guild; A bouquet for Grandma, Colour Library International (USA) Limited; Flowers for my sweetheart, Colour Library International (USA) Limited; Family keepsakes, Gerald Koser; Nostalgic treasures, Three Lions, Inc.; HANSEL AND GRETEL, Dennis Hockerman; GRANDPA'S KITE, John Slobodnik; Autumn scenic, South Woodstock, Vermont, Fred Sieb; Babcock Mill, West Virginia, Freelance Photographers Guild; COUPLE BEFORE FIREPLACE, George Hinke; THE HALLOWEEN PARTY, Frances Hook; inside back cover, Colour Library International (USA) Limited; back cover, Alpha Photo, Inc.